# A King's Love

## An Urban Love Story

### K. Jahmani

A King's Love

Copyright © 2016 by K. Jahmani

# Table of Contents

# Chapter One

Walking up the last few steps that led from the train platform to civilization, Bliss exhaled heavily. She was almost home; just one more block to walk from the train station and her long day would be over. She could not wait to get home, take a shower, put her feet up, and eat some Snicker's Ice Cream straight from the carton. Her day was not supposed to be this long, in fact, she expected this day to be a breeze.

Today was the day of her latest OB/GYN appointment. It was special, because she found out the sex of her baby. Even though she was tired, she was ecstatic that she got to see her baby girl and hear her heartbeat. A smile slowly crept its way to her face as she felt her baby move around.

It was supposed to be a special moment for her and her boyfriend of four years, Mario. However, Mario canceled saying that he was called into work at the last minute. To say she was disappointed would be an understatement, but sadly she was used to going through her pregnancy alone.

Rounding the last corner to her building, Bliss stopped into Lita's, the neighborhood bodega. She had a strong craving for some blue raspberry Now and Later's and a pineapple soda.

"Hey, Mami," Bliss said to Lita, who was sitting behind the candy made partition.

"Hey Junior."

"Sup, Ma, how you?" Junior was Lita's grandson that worked in the store every day to help his grandparents out.

"I'm doing a'ight, how you?"

"I'm good; you want the usual?" he asked in reference to the Ham and Cheese Hero Bliss got every afternoon.

"Si, baby girl been starving me all day. Make me feel like a bottomless pit and shit." she said laughing.

"Bebita? Es una niña?" Lita poked her head up from behind the register.

Bliss beamed as she answered Lita, "Si, mami. I found out a little while ago."

"Yeah, girl; I just left his sexy Puerto Rican ass. That nigga put a hurting on my pussy. Got a bitch walking funny and shit." a girl laughed obnoxiously loud into a pair of headphones. Her one-sided conversation was loud enough to interrupt Bliss and Lita. "Yes bitch, he begged for a piece of this cake, talm bout he called out of work for me." She paused while grabbing a bag of barbecue chips. "Exactly bitch, his lying ass. I ain't got the time."

Bliss felt like the side of her face was burning, so she turned to the side and peeped that the loud girl was staring at her. They made eye contact, but Bliss turned her attention back to Lita who was trying to hand Bliss her change.

"I'll see you later Lita, I'mma go and lay down before I start on baby girl's room."

The loud girl got behind Bliss in line and abruptly ended her conversation, "Aye, I'mma call you back." Bliss could feel that the girl was about to start some shit so she grabbed her shit and said her goodbyes. "Oh, it's a girl? Congratulations?"

Bliss looked over her shoulder with a confused look etched into her pretty round face, her hazel eyes showing her confusion. "Do I know you?"

"Nah, but ya man does." she said smirking.

Bliss raised her eyebrows and chuckled, "I'll be sure to pass your congratulations on." Turning back around, she diverted her attention back to Lita and Junior "I'll see youse, later." She chunked up the deuce smirking as she proceeded to walk to the exit.

"Hasta Luego, Mami." Lita said trying to break the uneasiness that permeated the air. "You ready?" she asked the loud girl. The girl paid for her items and waited as Lita slowly bagged her items.

Lita didn't want any drama coming to Bliss' doorstep; she felt for the young girl.

Bliss walked out of the store and walked a couple doors down to the entrance to her building. She wanted to smack the smirk off of that girl's face, but she had a baby girl to think about. Her blood boiled just thinking about the audacity of this bitch. Bliss had to give her her credit, though; she was a bold one.

Before she could reach the door, the girl called out,

"Why you walk away so fast?" She walked over to where Bliss was standing, "I just wanted to say congratulations and to tell you that I love what you've done to the baby's room. I think pink will be a nice touch, don't you?"

Bliss hauled off and punched the girl between the eyes. She then punched her in the throat before grabbing her hair and pulling the broad down to her height. Bliss was only 5'4 where that girl had to be close to 5'8. Those few inches made a difference in a fight, so Bliss did what she had to to beat that bitch's ass. After just a few more punches to the girl's face, Bliss was pulled off of the girl by Junior.

"Come on, Ma. Cut that shit out. You can't be pregnant and shit out here fighting, Esabella. Calm down." Junior said, calling Bliss by her middle name. When she was younger, she hated her first name so she always told everybody her name was Esabella, or Esa for short.

"Man, Junior, I'm not even trying to hear that shit, son. That bitch mad disrespectful. She jumped mad fucking stupid. She lucky she not all the way fucked up!! Wait till I see ya ass again bitch. Dead ass."

"Oh don't worry bitch, you'll see me again hoe! Just like ya fucking man; that nigga wake up in my bed every morning hoe."

"Yeah whatever, bitch. Don't let me catch ya ass bitch. I'mma fuck you up on sight."

"Man, Esa take ya ass in the house. Dead ass, son." Junior said, putting Bliss down in front of her door.

"Yeah, take ya pregnant ass in the house before you get hurt bitch!"

"And you shut ya pussy ass up Rasheeda. You just got ya retarded ass whooped by a pregnant chick that's almost a foot shorter than you, son. You should be the one tryna find somebody house to go into. You don't even live in this hood, Ma, so bounce." Junior said dismissing her. The crowd that gathered around cracked up laughing.

Bliss picked her bag up off of the ground and searched for her phone. After unlocking it, she placed a call to her best friend Letty. "Jim's hoe house, you got the dough we got the hoe."

"I need you; I just got into a fight with one of Mario's little hoes that wanted to jump stupid."

"I'm on my way."

"I'm leaving his ass this time, Let. I got to. I got a baby girl to think of now man. I can't be out here fighting these bitches, and I'm not bout to let no motherfucka stress me." Bliss vented.

"It's a girl?!!" Letty squealed through the phone. Bliss knew that Letty was probably jumping up and down. Bliss smiled a little at her friend's excitement. "I knew we were having Cielo and not a Junior." Letty said laughing. "But in all seriousness, B, I'm on the way."

"Bet."

After hanging up, Bliss marched her way into the building and up one flight of stairs, making her way down the hall to their corner apartment. How could he do this to her? The level of disrespect is catastrophic. Did she mean that little to him? After all, she's carrying his child, and she gave up four years of her young life for him.

She knew that he would cheat more often than not, but he never brought that shit to the house that they shared. He was on some other shit with this. And on top of all of that, he fucked that hoe in what was supposed to become their daughter's room.

They had a second bedroom that they would allow their guest to sleep in, but they took all of that out to start converting it to the baby's room. Bliss already had the design, the theme, and the furniture. The furniture was waiting at her dad's house; she just had to send for it when she was ready.

Walking into the house, and placing her bag on the table, Bliss went straight to their room. She could hear Mario down the hall in the bathroom taking a shower. Grabbing her oversized Nike duffle bag, she began throwing shit in there. She was a whirlwind as she began snatching clothes off of the hangers, and snatching the clothes from her drawer. She swiped all of her perfumes and jewelry into the bag. She grabbed a few pair of sneakers, sandals, and Timberland boots and threw those in the bag as well.

Bliss heard the shower cut off at the same time that she heard a horn blaring from outside. She walked out of the bedroom with her bag in tow and went over to the living room window.

"Rapunzel, Rapunzel, let down your bundles!" Letty yelled up to Bliss once she saw her in the window.

"Bitch you tried it! You know these inches mine." Bliss replied while laughing. "I'mma buzz you in; I need you to get my bag."

"Bet"

She buzzed her friend in and dragged her bag down the hallway and to the top of the steps. She pushed the bag down the steps to a waiting Letty. She straightened up and headed towards the apartment.

"B, where you going?"

"I have to get my purse. I left it on the table it has my wallet plus my sonograms of baby girl."

"A'ight, but hurry B. I don't feel like shooting nobody today." she said, her voice void of any humor.

Bliss knew that Letty was serious. "I'll be right back. It should only take a second."

She walked swiftly towards the apartment and entered. When she got in there, Mario was sitting on the couch with his elbows on his thighs. She took him in with her eyes. He was dressed casually in a white V-neck shirt, gray Polo sweatpants, and a pair of wheat-colored Timberlands. His face looked pinched, like he was thinking hard about something.

"So you leaving me?" he asked in an even tone.

"Fuck you, Mario."

"What you mean fuck me? Fuck I do to you?"

"First of all, you missed OUR baby's appointment today. I wasn't even tripping cause you said you had to work Mario! You left me hanging for some loose ass pussy. That's fucked

7

up, B." Her eyes watered at the pain she was feeling, but she refused to let him see her cry anymore.

"Stop raising your voice at me Bliss. I was at work, I told you they called me in."

"Since when was fucking a broad in our apartment in the room that's for your child a part of your job description? Huh Mario?"

"Whatchu talking about Bliss? I ain't smash no hoes." He tried but failed to maintain the smirk that played on his lips.

"Miss me with the bullshit, Mario. I just fucking fought that broad. You need to keep ya fucking hoes in check. It's bad enough that I know about your cheating, but for you to do that in my baby girl's room? In my house? Where I fuck you at? Where I rest my head and rub your feet at? You brought that bitch in my sanctuary, my castle. That mean, she's that much closer to my throne, and I'm not bout to fight no bitch over a man that don't even love me. Dead ass."

"Man, shut up all that hot shit you talking, Ma. I ain't bring nobody in here. And so what if I did? I pay all the bills up in this mufucka anyway. I moved you in here with me. This my shit."

"That's perfectly fine, Mario. You can have 'yo shit' and 'yo hoes'," she said, while using air quotation marks. "I'm out". She walked over to the table and grabbed her purse, checking to make sure that her sonogram pictures were in there. He got up from the couch and quickly made his way to her. Grabbing her around her waist, he backed her up into the wall.

She looked up at him and admired his sexy ass; that man was blessed. His caramel coffee complexion tied together his Puerto Rican and Black features perfectly. His goatee and thin mustache stayed freshly lined up. His black curly hair was in its natural state and hung just past his shoulders, framing his thick eyebrows and gray eyes. He reminded her of a darker version of Rick Gonzalez, the cute actor from 'Coach Carter'.

She studied his gray eyes, broad nose, and thick eyebrows. She looked at his plump lips as he licked them. Normally, her pussy would be aching with lust being this close to him. Today though, she was turned off. He really left her hanging and violated in a major way. He lowered his head to hers, leaning in for a kiss. Bliss ducked and pushed him off of her.

"Move, Mario."

"It's like that? You just gonna leave ya man hanging like that?"

"Fuck you mean leave you hanging? I've been with you since I was fifteen, man, and now I'm carrying your child. You left us hanging, Mario. You're supposed to be a man and take care of your family. I know you've been cheating on me, but I mean, don't your hoes know they place? I should have never been approached, especially while carrying your. Fucking. Child!" she clapped after each word for emphasis.

He closed the distance between them and lowered his lips until they were barely touching her ear. "You know you not leaving me, right?" He sucked her lobe into his mouth before biting it gently.

"Sssss," her hiss of pleasure slipped out before she could stop it. "Stop Mario, move."

"You really want me to stop, baby?" His lips found their way to her pouty lips. He kissed her, but she didn't return it. "Kiss me" She looked up at him defiantly but didn't utter a word. "I said kiss me Bliss!" He pulled her hair, snapping her head back, so he could control her movements.

"Let me go, Mario! I'm not fucking playing with your stupid ass, yo." His free hand found a way to the button on her jeans. "I said move!" she pushed him off of her again. She was taken aback when his open hand landed across her face.

"Man, Bliss, I keep fucking telling you about that shit. You always make me do that shit!" He punched the wall right next to her head, as she ducked out of the way and moved around him. "Why does it always have to end with me hitting you?" He heaved.

"Fuck you, Mario" she said walking towards the door again.

She had her hand on the doorknob when Mario grabbed her by the throat and slammed her back against the wall. Bliss was stunned silent as her breath lodged in her throat. Mario didn't let up as he started to swing wildly.

"You think you leaving me? I'll fucking kill you before you leave me." His punches were landing everywhere, her face, her chest, and unfortunately her stomach. Her body was tired,

and it hurt but she had to fight back. She tried to push him
back but to no avail and was met with a particularly harsh left
hook to the face. It knocked her to the floor where she curled
up in the fetal position. She tried to hang on. She knew that
Letty was outside and prayed that Let would figure out that
she was in trouble.

"Mario, please! Think about the baby! Mario!" she pleaded
but her cries fell on deaf ears. If anything, it seemed to make
the punches rain down harder. It was as if he was possessed.

A scowl was etched into his beautiful face and his eyes
looked void of any emotion as he repeatedly screamed, "I'll
kill you, before you leave me!" It was as if he was in another
dimension … another realm.

Her body couldn't take the beating anymore. She was
losing the battle against her closing eyelids. They were heavy,
but she had to fight. She knew that if she gave in she would
be surrounded by the darkness, a place she was all too familiar
with thanks to Mario. *Please let my baby be ok.*

Bliss was barely conscious when she heard a loud boom.
She didn't have the strength to look and see what it was. She
faintly heard commotion before the brutal attack abruptly
halted. *Thank God,* she thought before the darkness
succumbed her.

# Chapter Two

Letty was downstairs waiting in her cocaine white BMW. She was playing on her phone while waiting for her best friend of the last eight years, Bliss, to come downstairs from her apartment.

Letty tried to be patient, but it was coming up on a half hour since Bliss went back inside. If Bliss would've changed her mind, she would come downstairs and tell Letty what was up. Yeah, Letty would be saddened by the news, however she could understand. After all, she is a woman first, so she empathizes with Bliss. There was no telling how many times Letty called Bliss crying over Tyriq's sexy, chocolate, psychotic ass.

She watched as an all-black Range Rover pulled up in front of her. She tried to get a glimpse of who was in the car, but the tint on the windows was so dark that you would think that the windows were painted black. Their music bumped making the cars, including hers, thump right along with it. She had never seen this car before, especially not in Bliss' neighborhood. She continued gazing trying to figure out who the mystery person was.

Her phone dinged with a notification distracting her for a few minutes before she remembered the mysterious stranger.

When she looked up, the car was off and they were nowhere in sight. *Damn, I wanted to see if they were cute.*

After another agonizing five minutes, Letty could not sit in the car anymore. Letty reached for her .40 from under the passenger seat as she prepared to get out of the car. "Something ain't right, man. I can't just sit here." she said out loud.

She would feel a lot better if her boyfriend of two years, Tyriq, was here. Not that she was scared in any form or fashion, but it was just what if something really was wrong with Bliss? She wouldn't be able to carry Bliss down the stairs by herself. She pulled out her spare key and made her way inside the building, up the stairs, and down the hall towards Mario and Bliss' corner apartment.

*The fuck is that?* After hearing a strange noise, Letty sprinted the rest of the distance. When she made it to the door, she could hear Mario yelling incoherently. She didn't hear Bliss at all.

She hurriedly tried to find the right key to the door on her key ring and dropped them. "Fuck it." She aimed her gun at the lock and fired. The door opened instantly. When she entered the apartment, she saw Mario standing over a barely conscious Bliss kicking her repeatedly. Her body flashed with rage as she aimed at Mario and shot twice hitting him once in the shoulder and once in the leg.

"Fuck!" Mario screamed when he got hit. "You stupid bitch!" he fell to the floor gripping his shoulder.

"Fuck with me if you want to, Mario. The next one will be fatal." She rushed over to Bliss. Her heart dropped seeing her person all bloodied and battered. She checked Bliss' pulse and it was faint. "Fuck! I'm here, B. A'ight? I'mma be right back."

Letty got up from Bliss and went to kneel over Mario. She tightened her grip on the gun and pistol whipped him. She hit him repeatedly with every ounce of rage that she felt. "Fuck nigga!" she didn't take too long because her focus was Bliss. "Stay ya punk ass down!" She kicked him once more in his injured shoulder, and when he didn't move, she ran out of the apartment and into the hallway.

"Yo! I need help!" She banged on the neighbor's door. "Please! I need help!" Her banging increased as she became more and more frantic. The door flew open, and Letty was met with the barrel of a gun. She immediately stepped back and raised her gun. "Son, I don't want no problems. I just need some help."

A cute brown-skinned man about 6'2 stepped into the hallway. He towered over Letty's 5'4 frame. Tucking his gun away, he chuckled and smiled cockily.

"A'ight yo, you got it. You can put the shit away. I don't want no problems either, Ma." She lowered it but didn't put it away. She wasn't worried about the tall stranger; she held on to it just in case Mario thought that she was fucking around. "What's up shorty?"

Concern was etched into his features as he checked out her disheveled appearance. He looked down at her size seven

Timbs and saw blood on them. From there, he moved up to the blood that was on her bare knees and hands. Her face was void of emotion, ready for war, but her eyes gave her away. They were glossy and had this petrified look to them.

"My friend. I can't get her down the stairs; I gotta get her to the hospital. He almost killed her this time."

"Who?" the man was trying to follow along but she was speaking too fast.

"Look, I don't have time for twenty-one questions. You gonna help us or not?" Her fierce stare locked onto his confused one. He lifted his black Giants fitted and scratched his head before replacing his hat. He merely nodded, and she ran back inside of Bliss' apartment. "She's in here!"

He followed her panicked cry and went inside. He was not prepared to see a female scrunched in the fetal position in a pile of blood. He ran over to her immediately and picked her up.

"Take my keys out of my back pocket, yo." Letty ran over to him and followed directions. "A'ight, let's go." He was almost out of the door when something caught his eye. "The fuck? What about him?"

Letty followed his gaze and smacked her teeth, "Man, leave his ass here. He the nigga that did this shit."

When they were outside the building, Letty pressed the unlock button and the all-black Range from earlier lit up. *So he is cute,* she thought as she ran over to the truck and opened the back door for him. After setting Bliss down, the man ran to the driver's side and peeled out.

"You gone be a'ight, B. I'mma make sure of it." Letty kissed Bliss' forehead as the stranger swerved through the city traffic.

\*\*\*\*\*

The rest of the day was a blur for Letty. The car ride, the blood, the crying of Bliss' parents. She saw it every time she closed her eyes. As soon as she got to the hospital, she called Tyriq and told him what happened. He dropped everything and came right away.

The man that helped her out left shortly before Tyriq got there. He said he would come back and check on them in a few; she didn't expect him too though.

*Lord, please just let my person live. I can't live without her.* Letty was so antsy and anxious that she just couldn't sit still. This had to have been the most agonizing time in her life. They'd been there for hours and the doctors still hadn't said anything. Letty approached the nurses' station and went to the nurse that had been giving her the run around.

"Man, I've been here for going on four hours, and you mean you can't tell me shit? Her name is Bliss Esabella Love, she's nineteen, date of birth July 5, 1996. What other information do you need? I need to know what's going on. What you want her blood type? Allergies? I mean shit, I gave you everything that you asked for the first time I approached you."

"I already told you that I don't have any information for you." the nurse rolled her eyes.

"Isn't that your job? To inform the family of what is going on? You can't even tell me if she in surgery, if her baby made it, or even if she stable or not. Ya ass don't know shit. You acting like you can't make a call or something. I mean, damn."

"I don't know what else you want me to do-"

Letty banged her fist on the counter before speaking "Why would I want ya incompetent ass to do something else for me, when you can't even do what the fuck I asked you to four hours ago." Letty rubbed her temples, a sign that she was about to lose it. She stalked away from the station before she ended up behind bars for bitch slapping that stupid nurse.

After watching Letty pace back and forth for the past twenty minutes, Tyriq stood up and grabbed Letty's hand. She snatched away, but he reached for her again. "Come with me."

"Where we going?" Her perfectly arched eyebrows furrowed with doubt.

"Just come on." He tugged her hand in an attempt to get her to move.

"Riq, I don't want to leave right now." She tried to tug her hand out of his grip, which caused him to squeeze tighter.

"I wasn't asking." She was about to object, but the look on his face made her reconsider. She really didn't have the energy to argue so she gave in and followed him onto the parking deck and into the back of his Black with red interior Cadillac Escalade.

He pulled out two blunts and a small bottle of Hennessey. He kept one on him for times like this. They didn't say anything … just passed the blunts back and forth while taking sips of the Henny. The normally lighthearted couple was down for the moment, each lost in their own thoughts.

Letty knew that she had to calm down and relax her nerves now, cause when she was allowed to see her better half, she wasn't going to leave her side, and she couldn't be by Bliss' side if she was locked up.

Tyriq's phone ringing unexpectedly scared Letty out of her daze. The blunt went out while she was daydreaming so she relit it. Those last few pulls had her right where she needed to be.

Tyriq ignored the call and turned his attention to Letty. "Come here." He grabbed her by her waist and sat her down so that she was straddling him. She placed her head in the crook of his neck while he rubbed her back softly. He kissed the small script tattoo going across the front of her left shoulder. It was his favorite tattoo of hers. Alright, so he may be a little biased seeing that the tattoo was of his name, *Tyriq Zymere*, but nonetheless, it was his favorite.

Tyriq was perfect for Letty. He calmed her crazy even though nine times out of ten he was the cause of it. Letty didn't know how she would find the strength to get up every morning if it wasn't for Bliss and Tyriq.

Letty had been through a lot in her short twenty-one years on this earth. Not everybody's life was a fairy tale. Someone had to live a hard life. She just chucked it up to being the hand that she was dealt. She could bitch about it or be about it and get it how she lived. What would bitching do?

Tyriq grabbed Letty's hair close to the scalp and pulled her head back gently from his neck. Once he could see her face, he attacked her lips. Letty melted against Riq, as he devoured her lips. He was pouring everything into this kiss, and she was hungrily accepting it. She broke the kiss first when her lungs couldn't take anymore.

Tyriq didn't stop; he began kissing and biting gently on her neck. Being this close with Letty always left Riq hard as a brick and with a need to be deep inside of her. Her soft moans were the only sound that could be heard in the car. The two blunts had both of them sensitive to the other's touch.

Tyriq snatched her tank top over her head in one fluent motion before cupping her 'C' cup breasts and flicking his warm, wet tongue over her budded nipples. "Oh, Riq" she moaned, while grinding down on his hard member. She could feel all of him through the thin material of his black basketball shorts.

"Take them shits off, Ma," he smacked her ass before grabbing the clip of the blunt out of the ashtray and lighting it. After stripping out of her jean shorts, Letty re-straddled his lap before removing his dick from his shorts. She wrapped her small, warm hand around his shaft and worked it up and down. "If you gone play with it, you better sit on that dick." he said before he grabbed her hair and pulled her close to him until his lips touched hers in a hungry kiss.

"Open," he commanded once they broke apart. She watched as he pulled on the blunt before barely touching his lips to hers. He blew the smoke slowly in her mouth before lifting her up and slamming her down on his dick. They groaned collectively at the contact.

"Ohhhh, shit" she gasped, cumming instantly.

"Mmhmm, give me that pussy, Ma." He licked her neck while slamming her down repeatedly. "Fuck!" he bit down on her shoulder blade. That sent her into overdrive; she couldn't take it anymore. She put her hand on his to slow him down, but he smacked it away. "Let that shit go, Letty." He bit down harder on her shoulder blade causing her head to fall back and her eyes to close as she rode him into a euphoric bliss. "That's right, Ma. Squeeze that dick."

"Oh yes, Daddy! Shit!" her mouth was slightly agape as her orgasm washed over her.

"Gah damn, this pussy wet." Tyriq was close, but never being one to be selfish, he wanted her to catch one more. He sat up and swiftly had her on all fours. Before she could process what was going on, he plunged deep inside of her from behind.

Letty tried to scream out, but her words got stuck somewhere along the way as he fucked her into oblivion. He pulled her hair back until her back was flush against his chest. "This my pussy, baby?" She merely nodded her head. "Un uh, you know better than that, Ma. Say it." He picked up his pace while he reached down and played with her sensitive bundle of nerves.

She moaned, "It's yours, baby."

He smacked her ass. "I can't hear you Let."

"Oh, shit! It's your pussy, baby. Fuck! I'm 'bout to cum again, Riq." He felt her pussy tightening up and start to convulse as he stroked harder to reach his peak.

"Let that shit go, baby girl." He bit down on her shoulder, as they climaxed together.

After catching her breath, Letty turned around and threw her arms around Tyriq's neck. She took a deep breath and let the tears that she had been holding in come out. Her heart ached; she felt helpless. She would give anything to switch places with Bliss.

After a few moments, Tyriq redressed Letty and himself before sitting back in the seat with her on his lap. He didn't say anything; he just pulled her closer and held her tight.

Besides Bliss, Tyriq was the only one that Letty could let her guard down completely with and cry in front of. Everybody else didn't know that that side existed.

Stroking her hair and rubbing her booty, Tyriq held Letty until she cried herself to sleep. He stretched out across his back seat and got comfortable with her laying on his chest before kissing her forehead and knocking out with her.

# Chapter Three

"Mwah," Bliss kept hearing a weird noise while feeling something wet on her face. She closed her eyes tighter and snuggled deeper into her pillow.

"Mwah." What the hell? she thought as she opened her eyes. She was met with a pair of gray dough like eyes, a cute button nose, and small, plump, smiling lips. Instantly smiling, she pulled the blanket back and stretched.

"Come here, silly girl." Bliss grabbed one-year-old Cielo and held her close before tickling her. The squeal of delight that she got in return made her heart seize in pure joy. Looking at her baby grinning caused a Kool-Aid smile to form on Bliss' face.

Sitting up, she pulled Cielo in her lap, buried her face in the baby's neck and sniffed. Feeling a sense of calm wash over her, Bliss whispered in her daughter's ear, "Eres mi Cielo en la tierra. You're my heaven on earth, pretty girl." Baby Cielo placed her chubby hand against her mother's face and babbled incoherently. Feeling content, Bliss closed her eyes and relished in the peace that this moment brought.

Suddenly, the room became very cold causing Bliss to shiver. Reaching for her blanket, panic began to set in as she realized that her arms were now empty.

"Cielo?!" she screamed, while throwing the covers every which way in search for her daughter. Where the hell is my baby? Jumping out of the

*bed, Bliss ran down the hallway and barged into her daughter's room.
"Cielo?"*

*When Bliss couldn't find her, she sprinted out of the room and
towards the living room. Running past the window, she saw a flash of
color. Going over to the window, she watched as Mario turned the corner
with Cielo while holding her hand as they walked up the block. Bliss
hastily ran out of the apartment and in the direction that she saw them go
in. She rounded the corner and sprinted full speed ahead.*

*"Mario! Give me my baby! Why are you taking her from me?
Mario!!" Hearing her mother's voice, Baby Cielo turned before snatching
her hand from Mario and running towards Bliss.*

*"Mama!"*

*"I'm here, baby girl," Bliss ran faster with her arms stretched out to
pick Cielo up. A smile spread across her face when she was within fifty
feet; she was almost there, just a little further to go.*

*Mario turned around and walked the short distance to Bliss. Her
smile instantly fell when she saw the menacing look on his face. Before she
could process what was happening, Mario kicked her in the stomach
causing her to double over in pain.*

*"Mama!" Cielo cried when Mario picked her up and began to walk
faster.*

*Bliss pushed her pain aside and went after them. She couldn't lose
her baby girl. She was giving it her all to get closer to them but it seemed
like, the harder that she pumped her legs, the further away he was.
"Mario!" She was in full blown panic mode now. Her heart thrashed
wildly against her ribcage as she poured everything into getting to her
daughter.*

# A King's Love

*A harsh, freezing cold wind blew by as it became instantly pitch black. It was so dark that Bliss couldn't see her hand in front of her face, let alone her daughter that she was still searching for. "Cielo," she cried, "I'm sorry baby." Falling to her knees in despair, she welcomed the darkness that surrounded her. "I tried to protect you."*

"Bliss, come on, Mami, you have to wake up now." Bliss heard a familiar voice call out to her. "You got ya rest now; stop being greedy." She heard the voice chuckle. "Come on open ya eyes; squeeze my hand or something."

Carlos was sitting in his youngest daughter's hospital room, watching helplessly as the machine breathed for her. This was the fifth day that she was in the hospital in a medically-induced coma, and she hadn't shown any signs of waking up yet. He hadn't left her side unless he was forced to by Letty. That was only payback from him forcing Letty to go home and rejuvenate. Grabbing her hand gently, he lowered his lips to it and placed a kiss on it. He put his feet up on the bed and got comfortable before placing their interlocked hands beside him and turning his attention to the T.V.

Opening her eyes, Bliss instantly closed them again. The room was so bright that it blinded her. Taking her time, the second time around, she slowly opened one eye at a time until they were adjusted. Looking around the room, she saw her dad sitting next to the bed holding her hand and watching T.V. She tried to talk, but when nothing came out, she realized that she had something in her throat. Starting to panic, she squeezed her father's hand.

His head snapped towards her, and he had a big smile plastered on his face, showing all thirty-two of his pearly whites. "Hey, Mami; you're up from your nap." She tapped the tube that was taped to her mouth in response. "Right, I'mma be right back." He left the room and returned with a nurse.

The nurse examined Bliss, checking over her face first. Her right cheek had a bruise on it, she had a small cut on her forehead, and her bottom lip was slightly split open. She had three fractured ribs and a sprained wrist.

Her eyes were almost swollen shut when she first got to the hospital, but the swelling went down over the last few days, and all that was left was the nasty blue-black color on her right eye.

After the nurse's examination, she stepped out to get the doctor, who determined that it was okay to take the breathing tube out. After the procedure was done, the nurse and doctor left, leaving Carlos and Bliss alone.

"Hey, Daddy," Bliss croaked out. He handed her a cup of water, "Thank you." After finishing the cup, he silently handed her another one. "How's the baby?"

He didn't say anything. He just watched her. He was so relieved that she was alive. If he never took his eyes off of her again, it would have been too soon. Carlos was distraught when Letty called him. He had to talk himself down from going to find Mario. His baby girl needed him right now, but he wouldn't rest until Mario was dealt with.

Bliss was starting to feel self-conscious under her father's intense stare. "You gonna say something, yo?" She grabbed onto the side of the bed and tried to sit herself up. A crippling pain shot through her body. She fell back on the bed, her hand shooting to her stomach.

"Yo relax, you gonna tear ya damn stitches out."

Her eyebrow's perked up, "Stitches?" Her heart dropped as she watched her father's face fall and his eyes water. "Daddy?" she whispered. His heart broke as he struggled to find his words. He knew that his daughter was going to be distraught.

"They had to perform an emergency C-section Bliss."

"An emergency C-section?" The tears started to pour down her swollen cheeks. "But I'm only twenty-four weeks," her panicked, hazel eyes met his in a questioning stare. His glossy, hazel eyes mirrored her agony as he solemnly nodded his head.

"I know." he choked out. "You suffered a severe placenta abruption. Meaning that your placenta separated from the uterus. You suffered a lot of trauma and lost a lot of blood, Esa. They said that they tried their best to get it under control and save you and … the baby."

"I lost my baby?" She felt like the world was snatched from under her feet. "That's – That's why I was leaving, Daddy. I- I was trying to protect her." It felt like there was an iron fist around her heart that was squeezing the life out of her. Every time her heart beat, it ached.

Carlos got up from his seat and gently wrapped his arms around his daughter. It broke his heart to see her so broken. "Ima find his ass, Don't worry about it."

She couldn't wrap her mind around the fact that she wasn't pregnant anymore. She had just felt her baby move. How could it be taken from her just that quickly?

After a few moments of silence, Carlos Kissed Bliss' forehead and put on Disney's *The Lion King* on his laptop. It was their tradition to watch it whenever one was having a bad day.

"Remember when I started my career?" Bliss grinned at the memory that her dad was bringing up. Carlos was a Paramedic and worked for the city.

She took in her father's smooth cappuccino features. His curly hair was cut short causing tight coils to form. Her father was a very handsome man with the most beautiful pair of hazel eyes that Bliss had ever seen.

"I would come home like four-thirty in the morning, and all I would see walking into the living room was the light from the T.V, a nest of curly hair, and big ole hazel eyes looking at me from under the blanket. Everyone else would be sleep and the house would be dark, and here you go, bright-eyed and bushy-tailed at four-thirty in the morning watching *Lion King* and shit," He grinned looking over at Bliss.

She giggled, "I would wake up and wouldn't go back to sleep without you. So I watched *Lion King*, It's our favorite movie."

"Yo, you had to have been about four at the time. Shit boi, I used to love walking in the door and seeing your big ole eyes staring at me. That got me through my rough nights, especially when I started working the night shift. Depending on which part of the movie it was, you might've been crying witcho punk ass."

"Shut up," she said laughing, "Mufasa is my nigga, and that bitch ass Scar did him dirty." Carlos barked out a laugh.

"Yeah, I hear you, I hear you. You still a punk, Esa." He was quiet as he relished in the memory. "That shit meant the world to me. Being exhausted from dealing with life and death all day, and then you come home and see the life that you made, the life that is a part of you, just waiting for you with a big ole smile, stale chips, and flat soda. It made being exhausted so much more worth it."

Just then, Letty came in bearing balloons, "You look horrible bitch."

Bliss cracked a small smile, "You don't even have on ya eyebrows or ya lashes hoe, so redirect that shit."

Letty laughed, "Don't say I don't love ya ass. Going a whole week without my bed and shit."

Bliss' eyes watered; she was so overwhelmed. She didn't know whether she was coming or going. She was trying to wear a smile and relish in the fact that her two favorite people were there with her, but she just couldn't shake the cloud that she felt hovering over her. Letty dropped her bag and the balloons on the couch that they had in the hospital room and made her way over to Bliss. Climbing in the bed carefully, she cuddled up next to her person, absentmindedly running her hand over Bliss' hair.

"Next time I shoot his ass, It's gonna be between the eyes." A giggle slipped out of Bliss as she looked over at Letty.

"Wait in line," Carlos said, his eyes glued to the laptop as Scar bitch slapped Sarabi.

"All youse is after me." Bliss chimed in.

"Respect," Carlos and Letty said in unison. They all laughed while watching Pumba dressed in drag.

The door creaked open and the room fell silent as Bliss' mom, Aria, and her boyfriend, Marcus, walked through the door. Bliss clung tighter to Letty when she saw him. Letty looked down at Bliss, "You a'ight?" she whispered in her ear. Bliss nodded her head; she didn't have the energy to argue. She prayed nobody made a big scene.

"Well, don't stop on our account." Aria marched over to Bliss and placed a kiss on her cheek. "Hello Bliss."

"Mother."

"You're not going to speak to Marcus?"

"Ma, don't start with me a'ight?"

"Why is he even here?" Letty spoke up. Bliss' eyes shot over to Letty's, pleading with her to let it go.

"I see we still haven't put the guard dog down."

"Watch ya mouth, Aria. Don't come in my daughter's hospital room with ya bullshit, son. This is not the time or the occasion."

"She's my daughter, too, Carlos. I can be here if I please."

Carlos waved his hand dismissively, "Not if you're going to be rude and disrespectful; she doesn't need that shit."

"Oh, so now you're Mr. Mom and knows what she needs? Fuck outta here, Carlos."

"Just take ya ass on somewhere, man. Like I said, my daughter doesn't need any added stress."

"Y'all come on, now. Please don't start." Bliss begged.

"Well, tell ya father to stop trying to argue with me." Aria rolled her eyes at Carlos.

"I ain't tryna argue with ya simple ass, so if you gonna be here, sit in that chair and shut up. I'm not gonna say this shit again."

"Yo, don't talk to her like that, my G." Marcus spoke up.

"I suggest you tell ya friend here to mind his business, cause I'm handling mine." *Aria better get this nigga if she wants him to keep breathing. My trigger finger already itching,* Carlos thought to himself as he looked over at Bliss.

Her whole demeanor changed once they walked in, and he didn't like that. He could tell that she was down about everything, which was understandable, but at least she had been trying to keep a smile on her face. However, since Aria and her punk ass boyfriend walked in, the small smile Bliss was sporting vanished.

"I'm a grown man, dawg. I can speak for myself. No need to speak through her, yo." Carlos didn't even look in Marcus' direction to acknowledge him. He kept his eyes trained on Aria.

"Aria," Carlos gave her an impatient look.

"Seriously, Carlos?" *He can't be serious right now.* Looking at Carlos' face, Aria could tell that he was not playing. She smacked her teeth and rolled her eyes. "You're really serious?"

Carlos didn't say anything else. He sat back in his chair with his hands behind his head with his eyes trained on the T.V. Sighing deeply, Aria got up and walked towards Marcus.

"Come take a walk with me, Marcus."

"Word, Aria? That's how you feel, son?"

"Just come on." She stretched her hand towards him, and he smacked it away.

"Fuck outta here with that bullshit, Man." He stormed out of the room with the door slamming behind him. Carlos watched with a distasteful look on his face. *Where did she get this pussy ass nigga from?*

"What Carlos?!"

"I ain't say nothing so watch how the fuck you talking to me, Aria. I should smack the shit out of you for the bullshit you just pulled. Ya daughter not comfortable around that man, and you gonna bring him up here like he a part of this family. It's F.O.E.," he said, tapping his chest over his heart. "Family Over Everything, unless you forgot that shit, too."

"Over course I didn't forget!"

32

"Well then, fucking act like it. First thing you ask ya kid to do is to say hello to ya pussy ass boyfriend. You supposed to be asking her how she is. She just woke up three hours ago from a coma, and you gonna bring this shit to her." Carlos got up and kissed Bliss on the forehead. "I'mma go to the crib for a little minute and get my mind right … take a shower and all that good shit."

"Yeah I ain't wanna say nothing, Daddy, but I could smell you from over here." Bliss said with a straight face. She watched as her dad's face fell in shock before she fell out in fit of giggles.

"I see how you do punk." he grinned at her.

"Carlos, can I talk to you outside for a moment?" Aria asked, grabbing her jacket and waiting by the room door.

"Nah son, you good." He walked over to where Bliss was and gave her a hug.

"I'll call you later, Bliss." Aria said looking over at Bliss waiting for a response.

"Bet." Bliss said uninterestedly. Aria rolled her eyes before storming out of the room.

"Can I smack her?" Letty asked rubbing her hands together.

"Down girl," Bliss giggled.

Carlos chuckled before kissing her forehead once more. "Yo, y'all be good a'ight? I'll be back here in a little while. I love you."

"I love you, too, Daddy."

*****

**Knock! Knock!**

Bliss looked at the door as it opened and saw Junior walking in with a book bag hanging off one shoulder. His Versace cologne greeted her before he could fully get in the door.

He had on a gold and black custom made 'Junior' baseball jersey. Down low, he wore black jeans and black Timbs with a gold and black snap back to top it all off.

His plump lips were pulled into a smile as their eyes connected. She smiled shyly in return. "Junior, what you doing here?"

He feigned hurt, "I came to check on you, yo. I can't check on my friend?"

She giggled, "You good, son. You can sit on the couch if you want. Letty might bitch when she gets back, but you know how that goes."

He smacked his teeth, "I ain't worried 'bout that little ass Chihuahua," He waved his hand dismissively before plopping down on the couch, while propping his leg up on the edge. "On second thought …" he started before hopping up from the couch and making his way to the chair that was posted beside Bliss' bed. "I'mma sit up here with you."

Once he was settled, he looked at Bliss and smiled. "You good, Esa?"

Bliss and Junior had known each other for the past four years. They met when Bliss started dating Mario. Junior's

34

grandmother, Lita, lived in the apartment right next door to Bliss and Mario.

Over the years, Bliss developed a personal relationship with Junior, Lita, and Lita's husband and Junior's grandfather, Vernon.

Bliss focused on the T.V, "I'm a'ight."

"I would've come by sooner, but I know you just woke up a couple days ago, and I wanted to give ya family some time, ya feel me?"

Junior gently placed his warm hand on her face, then turned her head towards him. He just looked at her for a few moments before removing his hand from her cheeks.

"You good; this is a welcomed surprise." she smiled gently.

"I got something for you." he started after he settled back into his chair.

"Oh, word?"

"You know how I do," he smirked. He leaned over and picked up his book bag from its spot on the floor beside his chair.

A smile instantly spread across Bliss' face as she watched him pull out a brown paper bag. "You didn't."

"Who didn't? I figured they got you eating this nasty ass hospital food and shit, so I brought you a little something to brighten your day." Handing her the bag, he stood up and swung his bag onto his shoulders.

Bliss' face fell when she saw him stand up. "You gone?"

Noticing the disappointment on her face, Junior chuckled, "Nah, so put ya lip in. Here, put this on; I'mma be right outside so you can change." He placed a pile of clothes on the bed and took the brown paper bag from her.

"Where we going?"

"I'll be outside, Esa."

Accepting defeat, Bliss waited until Junior was outside before looking at the clothes that he put on the bed. She picked up the black maxi dress and ran her fingers over the soft material.

*I know this isn't from my closet,* she thought, as her eyes landed on a tag hanging off of the dress. She checked for a price, but the price was conveniently non-existent. *Hell no, I can't accept this.*

Bliss was about to take the dress back to Junior. She was in her head about him buying her something. Why would he even buy her something in the first place? Especially something this nice. He must want something. She had never known a nigga to do something so nice for her without wanting something in return.

"Yo, you ready yet, Ma?" Junior yelled through the door, while knocking.

Shaking her thoughts away, Bliss slowly sat up, "Yeah, almost done." she yelled back. Her body was still very sore, especially her abdomen. She gently pulled her hospital gown off and slid the soft cotton material over her swollen stomach.

Her heart ached at the passing thought of her baby girl. Sighing deeply, she forced herself to the edge of the bed. She sat there for a minute to get the strength to get out of bed. Feeling overwhelmed with emotions, Bliss let the tears fall. Her whole being ached with sadness, and she felt like her body was made of lead. Every move she made exerted all of her energy.

"A'ight, come on Bliss, pull it together, yo," she coached herself out loud. After a few more tears and a couple of deep breaths, she wiped her face and put her curly hair up into a sloppy bun. Then, she slid her feet into her plush Nike slides before meeting Junior in the hallway.

"Your chariot awaits." Junior waved his hand in front of a wheelchair. Despite her mood seconds earlier, Bliss laughed as he helped her sit down.

They were quiet as Junior walked them down different hallways, making turns. "If I didn't know any better, I would say that you were lost."

"Nah, I got this, Ma." he said, as they stopped in front of an elevator. The elevator opened, and they got on. "Trust me." Once they were off, Junior parked the wheel chair and gently lifted Bliss up in his arms bridal style.

"I texted Letty telling her that I'm with you, so if I die, she's shooting you first."

Junior barked out a laugh, "Yo, you OD'ing; I aint gone hurt you, Ma."

"I can walk ya know."

He stopped in front of a door, "I know; I just wanted to hold you," he winked. He walked through the door before Bliss could respond. Her smart response was stuck in her throat as she looked around in awe. He took them to a roof top garden that was created a few years ago on the tenth floor of the hospital. They weren't on the actual roof, just in the center of all the buildings that the hospital was made up of.

There were waterfalls and beautiful, colorful flowers that filled Bliss up with a sense of peace. She took in the green grass and the trees that surrounded her.

Junior walked them over to one of the many benches in the shade and sat her down before getting settled himself. From where they were sitting, she had the perfect view of the waterfall that she was in love with.

"Oh, wow," Bliss stated in admiration. "This is so beautiful. I didn't know this was here."

"It's a well-kept secret," Bliss playfully punched him, causing him to grab his arm and fake hurt. "What you do that for, yo?"

"Cause you ain't tell me about this being here."

"I don't have to tell you everything, Ma." he said smirking. "Some shit you gotta take to ya grave, ya feel me?"

"Yeah, I hear that hot shit you spitting, boi" she smiled. "So how'd you know this was here? It's so peaceful."

"You mad nosey," he barked out a laugh when she pushed him on his shoulder. "Nah, but I used to bring my granddad

out here when he got sick and shit." Junior cleared his throat
before shifting uncomfortably.

"Thank you; it's so serene here." she stated, changing the
direction of the conversation.

"You're welcome, Ma." He smiled at her.

After a few more moments in silence, Junior pulled out
two brown paper bags and handed one to Bliss. She looked
inside as she mentally did a happy dance.

Tears sprang to her eyes, as she pulled out a hero, a pack
of blue raspberry Now & Later's, and a pineapple soda.
Before she could stop them, a few rolled down her cheeks.

These were the items she ate almost every day when she
was pregnant with Cielo. She felt overwhelmed with sadness,
but also appreciation because Junior didn't have to do any of
this. It was like a raging war between the two emotions.

"Why you crying?" Junior reached out and wiped the tears
away gently with his thumb.

Bliss looked up at Junior through blurry vision and cracked
a small smile, "It's the hormones; every small thing makes me
cry." He looked worried but didn't question her further.

They made small talk as they ate and enjoyed their
surroundings. Their laughing and joking around with each
other had Bliss feeling carefree, even if just for the moment.
She hadn't laughed so much except for with her dad and
Letty.

When she was with Mario, it was like she had on blinders.
She didn't see anyone but Mario. Even after the abuse, the

cheating, and the fighting other girls, Bliss never lost sight. She remained faithful and loyal to him and look where it landed her.

Junior had been around, but she never paid much attention before. After today her interest was piqued. She wasn't anywhere ready or remotely close to being ready for dating but she could definitely use a friend, and Junior seemed like a perfect candidate.

# Chapter Four

"FUCK!" Bolting straight up in bed, Bentley placed his hand over his rapidly beating heart. "It was just a fucking dream." After a few deep breaths, his heart rate slowed to a minimum.

He turned on the lamp that was sitting on an end table, next to his king sized bed. Grabbing his IPhone off of the table, he padded his way to the kitchen in his two-bedroom condo. He made himself a cup of water before checking his phone for any missed calls.

One stood out the most, so he called them back immediately.

"Yo!" they answered on the first ring.

"Damn, nigga. I thought you forgot about ya brother. A nigga been home a little over three months and ain't heard from you." Bentley stated.

"That's my fuck-up. It's been some wild shit going on, my G. I'm just tryna get it handled. I ain't wanna bring it to ya doorstep ya feel me?"

"Yeah, I feel you. Respect. So what's good Riq?"

"You coming out with us tonight?" Tyriq asked Bent.

"Us? Who all going?" Bentley made his way to the favorite part of his condo ... the large windows that gave way to a beautiful view of his city's skyline.

"My girl Letty and her best friend Bliss. It's Bliss birthday, so we bout to be lit. Be ready by nine-thirty; we going to Fantasy."

Bentley looked over at the brightly lit clock on the cable box. It read eight forty-five. "Gah damn, nigga. I'll just meet y'all there."

"A'ight, nigga. I see ain't much shit changed in four years with ya slow turtle, molasses moving ass." Tyriq laughed.

"I bet I'm fast enough to fuck yo bitch." Bentley retorted.

"But are you fast enough to outrun this foot I'mma put in yo ass."

"I did it before, I guarantee I'd do it again." Bentley responded casually.

"Yeah, a'ight; I hear you. Witcho high yellow ass."

"Yo, ole unoriginal, overly used, old jokes telling ass. You need to find some new material son."

"Yo bitch wasn't saying that the other night, nigga." Tyriq responded.

"Yo, ya ass rusty, Riq." Bentley said while laughing, "Done fell off since the kid ain't been around, huh?"

Riq smacked his teeth, "If you don't get ya pissy-colored ass the fuck off my line nigga." Tyriq laughed.

"A'ight, nigga. I'll be through."

"Bet." Tyriq said.

"One." Hanging up the phone, Bentley made his way to his bedroom, where he connected his phone to the surround sound speaker system he had throughout the house. After finding the right music playlist, he headed to the en-suite bathroom and started the shower before going to his walk-in closet.

Bobbing his head and rapping along to "1/4 Block" by Jeezy, Bent rolled a few blunts before lighting one and finding something to wear. He settled on a black with red lettering Chicago Bulls' jersey, black cargo shorts, a matching Bulls' snapback and his 'Bulls Over Broadway' Jordan 10's.

After finishing his first blunt, Bentley got in the shower. Since he got home from prison, he always spent a long time in the shower, and he appreciated every hot minute of his shower, but since he was on somewhat of a time limit, he kept it less than forty-five minutes this time.

Wrapping the towel around his waist, Bentley froze as the music paused. He heard a noise coming from the living room causing anxiety to creep up his spine as he reached for his piece that he stashed in the bathroom. Taking the gun off of safety, he eased the door open and stepped out into his bedroom.

He saw that the portable dock for his speaker system was gone, and his phone was laying by itself on his dresser. After double checking to make sure his room was clear from intruders, he eased the bedroom door open and slowly made his way down the hall.

The music started back up and "Angel" by Anita Baker began to play throughout the apartment. As he got closer to the living room, he could smell cigarette smoke. He was no longer alarmed, knowing exactly who it was.

"How do you know where I live?" Bent asked to make his presence known. He found the intruder standing in front of the large windows in his living room.

"Do you really have to ask me that, Bent?" She turned around to face him. "A gun? Seriously, Bentley King?"

"Well, that's usually what happens when someone breaks into your house." He lowered the gun but kept the safety off.

"What's a mother to do when her son completely shuts her out?" Kat, Bentley's mother, asked before puffing on her Newport.

"You can show ya self to the balcony to finish that bogie." he stated before walking back to his room and throwing on a pair of basketball shorts. He grabbed a blunt and headed back to the living room.

He found her in the same spot, the cigarette now put out. He stood by the kitchen island and lit his blunt.

"Put that shit out, Bentley."

"You're more than welcome to leave. I'm sure you know the way out, since you found your way in."

"I didn't come here to go back and forth with you, Bent."

"Then, why are you here?" Bentley pulled from the blunt, as he went to the freezer and pulled out a bottle of Henny.

"I just wanted to see your face … see that you were okay and well. I worry about you, Bentley."

"Now you worry about me? I was in that prison for how long? And not once did you show ya face." Bent downed his first shot of the night. He welcomed the burning sensation as it spread warmth through his body. It chased the hurt that was radiating in his heart away. He quickly downed a second shot.

"Not visiting you doesn't take the worry away, Baby Ben." She called him by the childhood nickname she and his father used to call him. He smacked his teeth at hearing the old pet name, but chose to ignore it further.

Kat reached for her pack of Newport's until she remembered he didn't want her smoking in there. Not wanting to upset him further, she put them in her purse.

She put her hand out signaling that she wanted the blunt. He raised his eyebrows questioning her. She cocked one back, and he passed her the blunt.

His eyes roamed over his mother's chocolate skin from head to toe. This was the first time he had laid eyes on her in over four years. Nothing had changed about her; she even smelled the same. He wanted to go over there and scoop her into the biggest bear hug of all time, but his pride and pain wouldn't let him.

"You ain't even answer my calls, Ma. My letters went unanswered. There was nothing. That's fucked up, no matter how you spin it."

Kat was quiet as she passed Bent the blunt back. What could she say? No matter what she said, it wouldn't matter.

She looked in her son's handsome face and saw the anger, hurt, and confusion written all over it.

"You found your way in, you can walk yourself out. I got shit to do. Be safe." After kissing her on the forehead, he walked off down the hallway towards his room.

Hearing his door slam shut, Kat hung her head in disappointment. She had a long way to go to win her Baby Ben back. She already lost one Benny; she couldn't lose this one.

\*\*\*\*

Hearing the front door close, Bentley continued to get dressed. His head was reeling with thoughts.

He spent the last four years doing time for something that he didn't do, and for a person that shitted on him while he was locked up. Crazy thing is, he didn't regret it and would do it again if he had to.

What kind of man would he be if he let his mother even step one toe inside of a prison? Especially if he had the power to stop it?

Pushing everything to the back of his mind, Bentley did his final touches as he put on his two gold chains, sprayed his cologne, and placed his snapback on over his crinkly dreads that hung just below his shoulders. After double checking to make sure that he had everything, he left his apartment and headed towards his night out on the town.

Smoking a blunt, Bentley swerved in and out of the city's traffic in his all-black Range.

He briefly remembered the two girls he helped a few months back. He never did get a chance to go see the girl in the hospital. With everything happening so fast, he never found out either of their names.

He did go back up there a few hours later, but he didn't recognize any of the women in the waiting room as the girl that pointed the gun at him. He prayed that the girl that was beaten survived. He hadn't seen her around his grandmother's apartment building, not that he'd be able to recognize her, but he just hoped that that was a positive sign.

Shaking his head to clear the morbid thoughts, Bentley turned the music up and rapped along to "Really Really" by Kevin Gates.

Approaching his destination, Bent observed how the line wrapped around club Fantasy. He pulled up to the curb, threw his Range in park, and hopped out.

"Don't scratch my shit," he said to the valet attendant after handing him thirty dollars.

Walking towards the entrance, he noticed all eyes on him. The girls had lust, and the niggas had envy, and Bent didn't give two fucks about either. He knew he looked good and didn't need no thirsty hoes telling him so.

Standing at 6'2 with an athletic body and broad shoulders, Bentley was as fine as they came. His peanut butter complexioned skin, succulent plump lips, and slightly slanted, dark brown eyes mixed with his naturally two-toned dreads, were a deadly combination. His medium stubble framed his lips with precision tying all his features together perfectly.

Bentley walked past the long ass line and went right up to the bouncer. "Big Black, what's poppin', Nigga?"

"Yo, what's up, Bent? Long time no see, youngin." Big black was 6'7, 350 pounds, and black as midnight. He used to run with Benjamin, or Benny, Bentley's father back before he was killed.

"I been around; Just low-key." Bent said dapping Big Black up.

"I feel you, youngin. With how shit went down with Benny, that's the best bet. Can never be too careful."

"Facts, OG. Anyway, let me get in here. You seen, Riq?"

"Came through not too long ago with his girl. Has a new girl with him, too. Shorty fine than a mufucka. Long hair, thick hips, perfectly round little ass." Big Black bit his lip, "Let me had been a few years younger."

Bentley barked out a laugh, "You stay wilding, son. Sit yo old ass down before you have an aneurysm or some shit."

"Fuck you, Bent," Big Black laughed.

"I'll holla at you before I dip, OG."

"A'ight, one."

The club was packed, dark, and cloudy. Bentley was swimming through the sea of people as he made his way to the opposite side of the club towards the stairs that lead up to the VIP lounge. Feeling the vibration from the bass of the music, Bent vibed along to the song blasting over the speaker.

Not watching where he was going, he bumped into a girl. "Oh, shit!" he yelled over the music as his arms shot out to catch her before she hit the ground. He was taken aback by the electricity that jolted through him when he made contact with her skin.

He watched her sexy, plump, and juicy lips move for a while before he realized that he couldn't hear what she was saying. Shorty had to be almost a whole foot shorter than him.

Tightening his hold that he had on her waist, he leaned down until his lips were barely touching her ear. "I couldn't hear you, Ma. You mind repeating it for me?" he said seductively in her ear.

He felt her shudder against him before she wrapped her hands around his neck until his ear was level with her soft lips. "I said, watch where you going next time. You stepped on my toes."

He pulled back to look at her face and cracked up laughing at how serious her expression was. She was pouting … bottom lip poked out, eyebrows furrowed, and the whole nine. Her expression was a total contrast to the feistiness in her voice. He had the uncontrollable urge to bite her lip, but instead, he laughed before bending down again.

"I'm sorry, shorty; it won't happen again." he said.

"It better not or you paying for my next pedicure."

He chuckled deeply in her ear before responding, "You got it, Ma."

She rolled her eyes, "My name ain't, Ma." She said before removing herself from the hold that he had on her.

Stepping away, she turned and tried to walk away. He gently grabbed her arm mid-step. Stepping up behind her, he let go of her arm and placed his hands on her waist.

"Where you going?" he asked her.

"I'm sure I'll see you around." He chuckled, hearing the smirk in her voice.

He spun her around so that she faced him "Can I at least get ya name, beautiful?"

"I'm Esa. And you?"

"I'm Bent. So check this, Miss Esa. I'm not quite ready to let you go yet. You mind having one dance with me?"

"Just was waiting for you to ask me," she smirked.

Bentley didn't miss a beat as he gently grabbed her hand and turned her around just as "Liquor" by Chris Brown bumped over the club's speakers.

He watched as her hips started to whine slowly to the smooth beat before stepping behind her and falling in sync with her fluent movements. He planned on talking to her during this moment. However, his words were forgotten as their bodies moved together. It was as if they were in their own little world.

Esa turned around to face him as she swayed to the music. When they locked eyes, Bentley got lost in her hazel pools. Stepping closer to her, he wrapped his arms back around her waist, stopping right above her plump ass. Their eyes stayed locked as they tried to become one on the dance floor.

Bentley was confused yet intrigued about the captivating hold she had on him. He was about to say fuck his boys and just leave with her. He had to find out more about shorty, and the club wasn't what he had in mind as the spot to do it.

"Es! Let's go; I've been looking for you, yo." Before Bentley could comprehend what was going on, he couldn't feel shorty thick hips in his hands anymore. He looked up as she was being dragged away by what he assumed was her friend.

He started following after them, but lost them in the sea of people. *I'mma see her little ass again.* he thought to himself, as he made his way towards the stairs. He pushed the thoughts of Miss Esa to the back of his head … for now.

Walking up the last couple of steps to the VIP, Bentley was caught off guard when he heard "Welcome home, Bent!!" being yelled and flashes from cameras going off.

He froze mid-step as he took in his surroundings. Only his closest friends and family were there. There were a few people that he didn't know, but Tyriq did say that this was his girl's best friend birthday party. He took notice that his brother was not there, but he didn't expect for him to be.

Pushing the thoughts of him and his brother's fallen relationship to the back of his mind, Bentley made his rounds and greeted everyone. They all either gave him a couple of grams, or bottles of Henny. Nobody showed up empty-handed.

After a couple of shots with his boys, he stepped outside on the patio for a minute. Always one for solitude, Bentley didn't do big crowds very well. He'd rather sit back and observe than to be in the mix.

"Welcome home, Bent!" Tyriq said, grabbing him into a brotherly hug. This was the first time that they had seen each other in four years without a glass separating them. Riq held Bentley down when he was upstate. He came to visit, kept him updated on the business, and kept money on his books.

"Preciate this, fam," Bent said once they separated. "I thought this was a birthday party, yo?"

"It's a party celebrating two important people. If I told you what it really was, you would not have come."

Bent fell out laughing, "You probably right."

"Nigga, ain't no probably about it. Yo ass wouldna came."

"A'ight my G, you right." Bentley took a swig of Henny as Tyriq lit up the blunt.

"Yo, I met this fine ass shorty on my way up here."

"So that's what was taking yo Mexican ass so long." Riq said while passing the blunt.

"Fuck you, nigga. You know I'm not Mexican."

"Listen, nigga, you mixed with a lot of shit. I can't keep up with that shit."

"You act like that shit gone change, yo." Bentley said through laughter and weed smoke. Bentley's mother was a

52

brown-skinned black woman but they were not one hundred percent sure what she was because she grew up in the system. Bentley's father was Black and Dominican.

Riq smacked his teeth, "Back to this shorty man."

"Right." Bent passed the blunt back and took a sip of Henny before continuing, "So I knock her over on accident. Nigga was zoning to Future and shit and ain't see her little ass."

Tyriq burst out laughing, "I swear, I almost knocked my girl teeth out zoning." Riq pulled from the blunt before passing it, "Where shorty at?"

"Fuck if I know, yo. We was fucking the dance floor up, then I look up and her Tasmanian devil looking ass friend pulled her away."

"What's her name?" Before Bent could answer, Tyriq's phone went off. "Aye, hold on a second. I gotta take this shit man."

"You good. I gotta take a leak. I'll be right back." Bent said to Tyriq, but he was already walking off with his ear pressed to the phone.

Bent made his way back inside and down a dimly lit hallway towards the bathroom when he heard yelling.

"Esa! Will you slow down. I'm tryna talk to you!" He turned around, interest piqued from hearing Esa's name, and saw two girls walking towards the girls' restroom. One was in the front walking hastily, while the other was trying to keep up. "You had me scared; I was looking all over for you. I didn't know what happened to you."

"Leave me alone, Letty! I'm not fucking twelve a'ight? I can handle myself."

"Well, how's that working out for you so far, huh? Last time I checked, your self-preservation skills weren't on one hundred."

Esa stopped mid stride and turned to look at Letty in disbelief.

"Shit, Es. I'm, I'm sorry," she slurred.

"Fuck you, Let." She had to get away from Letty before she lost her cool and punched her best friend in the face.

When Bliss turned back around she was face to face with Bent. She smiled a little despite her blood boiling. She stepped closer to him and pulled him down so she could whisper in his ear, "Can you get me out of here?"

He smirked down at her, "Just was waiting for you to ask me."

# Chapter Five

Wiping the steam from the shower in her bathroom at her and Letty's house, Bliss admired herself in the mirror. Her body healed well over the last few months. She loved what her pregnancy did to her body. Her hips widened and her ass got a little fatter, making her clothes tighter in all the right places. Her skin stayed cleared up and maintained the small glow that she developed.

She rubbed her scar that she got as a result from the C-section. She didn't know whether to hate it or to love it. On one hand, it was just a painful reminder of losing her daughter.

On the other, it was the only thing she had remaining from her pregnancy. The only trace that her daughter ever existed, aside from the one sonogram picture that she had left.

The sonogram she had was the one from when she first found out that she was pregnant. The one she lost was the one revealing the sex of Cielo. She looked all over for it, but couldn't find it.

Walking through the adjoining door that led to her bedroom, Bliss dropped her towel before she plopped down on her queen-sized bed. She scooped up some coconut oil and mixed it with her Endless Weekend body lotion, before massaging it into her body.

Closing her eyes and massaging her shoulders vigorously, Bliss inhaled deeply and exhaled slowly. Today was her birthday, but it felt like just another day. If she had it her way, she would be curled up in bed, watching Netflix on her TV, and eating whatever the hell she wanted.

She was going out tonight with Letty and Tyriq, and Bliss wasn't really a club person, but she did love to dance. She thought about just canceling, but she knew that Letty would drag her out of the apartment by her stilettos, kicking and screaming if she had to.

Bliss slipped her black bra and thong on before slipping an oversized t-shirt over her wrapped hair and down her body.

Blasting Rihanna through her Bluetooth speakers, Bliss danced in place as she started on her makeup. She was a natural beauty, so she didn't apply that much makeup. Just enough to accentuate what was already there.

After applying black eyeliner to both the bottom and top lids, Bliss applied her mascara to her medium-length eyelashes. Finishing off her makeup, she applied her Ruby Woo by Mac matte lipstick. It made her lips pop without making them look like they were about to fall off her face. She loved what this color did to her full lips.

Her phone ringing scared her straight from performing the new twerking trick she learned on the wall. Quickly recovering from the scare, she answered Junior's FaceTime call.

"Gah damn, girl; you can't just throw that beauty up on a nigga like that. You gotta warn me first." Junior said as soon as the call connected.

Bliss giggled as she sat down on the purple plush rug in her bathroom, "Hello to you, too, Junior." She admired his sexy, golden brown skin and pearly white smile. He took off his snap back revealing his Caesar cut with waves so deep Bliss swore she was lost at sea.

After scratching his head, Junior placed his hat on backwards.

"Happy birthday, Celie," he laughed.

She dropped the phone face down on the rug, "Shut up, nigga. Don't be talking about my head scarf."

He smacked his teeth, "Can you take me out of time out? Pick me up, nigga!"

She giggled before picking her phone up off of the rug. "Such a baby."

Junior laughed, "You miss me yet?"

Bliss watched through her screen as Junior stretched out on the couch that he was sitting on. "Nah," she said with the corners of her mouth turned up a little.

"I know ya big headed ass miss me. It's a'ight; I miss you, too, Es."

"How's the A? You gonna start saying Shawty and shit?" she laughed.

"You not funny, punk," he laughed. "You act like I'mma be gone forever. I'll be back in a couple weeks. I just gotta take care of business, ya feel me?"

"I feel you. Handle ya business." Bliss kept it short to hide her disappointment. Junior and Bliss had become really close over the last few months; he was an integral part of her day. He always had her going with him places in order to keep her out of the house, even if it was just a trip to the corner store.

He had to go on a business trip to Atlanta for a few weeks. What kind of business it was, she didn't have a clue. She was curious but never pried. She figured if he wanted her to know he would tell her. It wasn't a regular nine to five, that was for sure.

"So what's the plans, birthday girl?"

"Letty's making me go out to club Fantasy or some shit."

"That's what's up, Es. Try to have a good time. It's not gonna be that bad." Junior said smiling. "When I get back, we gonna celebrate forreal and do something you want."

"Go-kart racing!" she said excitedly.

"A'ight I got you." he smiled genuinely at her. She smiled back as they fell into a comfortable silence. After a couple of minutes, Bliss got up and went to her dresser where she got the second half of a blunt from earlier. "Just be careful tonight, Esa."

"I will be. No worries." Inhaling, she relaxed and let go of her nerves. "You going to sleep anytime soon?"

"I doubt it. You know how I do."

"Yo ass probably going to somebody strip club." Junior busted out in laughter. "Smack some fat asses for me," Bliss said seriously.

"You already know I got you. Have fun tonight with yo sexy ass."

"Boi bye, get off my phone," she said smiling at him.

"Yeah, I hear you. I'll talk to you, Esa. Be safe."

"You too, Junior." Ending the call, Bliss smoked the rest of her blunt in peace.

She hated being by herself, but she didn't have the energy or tolerance to deal with anyone. She barely dealt with Letty.

Since everything happened, it was like Letty grew into a mother bear. She treated Bliss like she was her child, and Bliss was feeling suffocated. It was bad enough that she couldn't escape the thoughts and flashbacks that replayed relentlessly in her mind, but to have your best friend constantly on your back about every little thing was overwhelming. She couldn't even pee without Letty breathing down her neck.

Walking back into the bathroom, Bliss found her way into the mirror. She couldn't help but allow her thoughts to roam to those of her baby girl. Her due date would have been in a few weeks. She thought her life would be so different at this point, preparing for the arrival of Cielo. Some days, she didn't know if she was coming or going.

Bliss' chest began to hurt, and she felt a headache coming on. It felt as if someone was sitting on her heart and lungs making it so she couldn't breathe. Flashbacks and memories started to bombard her psyche … visualizations of her last ultrasound, the fight with that dumb bitch, the countless times Mario beat her.

Sitting up, she began to break down some weed for a couple blunts as she tried to push the thoughts to the back of her mind.

The thought of never meeting her daughter properly slammed into her like a ton of bricks. She wanted to hold her baby … feel her move around inside of her. She just wanted to give her kisses and hear her cries. Bliss yearned to hug her … to feel the warmth of her daughter's smooth skin flush against her own.

She prayed to hear her baby's heartbeat again.

Bliss walked to the kitchen and grabbed one of her personal birthday bottles of peach Ciroc out of the freezer. She grabbed a yellow can of Red Bull out of the fridge and cup out of the cabinet before padding back to her room.

She took four shots back to back. Only thing she used to chase them were pulls from her blunt.

Exhaling, she felt the pressure that was building up disperse. The memories disappeared, and she could breathe again. Bliss relaxed completely and let the effects of her high take place.

\*\*\*\*\*

Bliss gave herself a once over in her full-length mirror. She had to admit, even though she wasn't feeling the best, she looked damned good. She wore a black halter crop top and a

black high waisted, double split maxi skirt that smoothed over
her thick curves and ass.

There was not a hair out of place. Her smooth and silky
mane was straight down her back. She had her bangs curled to
the side covering her right eye. Her baby hairs were slicked
down and 'on fleek' as Letty would say. The sideburn of her
edges curled up from the gel and edge control leaving a petite
coil. She added a few gold bangles, a pair of door knocker
gold hoops, and a simple gold chain to complete her look.

The buzzing from her cell phone distracted her from her
look-through in the mirror.

"Hello?" she answered. Sitting down on the bed, she
began to put on her gold Giuseppe Zanotti pumps.

"Hey, Mami. Happy birthday!" Bliss smiled as her dad's
voice poured over the phone making her instantly cheer up.
She had been waiting for his call all day.

"Thank you, Daddy"

"I'm sorry I couldn't call you earlier," Carlos started, but
Bliss stopped him.

"It's okay, Daddy. I'm just happy to hear your voice."

"How you doing, baby girl?"

"I'm ok." Bliss said walking to stand in front of the
mirror's dresser.

"I'm not gone lie; I'm a little worried about ya. But then
again, I guess I wouldn't be a good father if I didn't worry.
Yo, before I forget sweetheart, did you hear from ya sister?"

"She Facetimed me and let me speak to Angel earlier today."

"That's good. I thought maybe she told you about the cookout on Sunday."

"What cook-out?" Bliss asked.

"Since I had to work all day yesterday and we couldn't have the Love's Annual 4th of July cookout, I'mma do it on Sunday. So bring a side dish."

"Okay, I'll bring something."

"I haven't heard from you in a little while." Carlos said, his tone depleting.

"I-I know, Daddy. I just uh- I just gotta figure some stuff out first ya know?"

"Nah, I don't know Bliss. I'm really trying to understand, Mami but I don't get it. I'm ya father, and I ain't seen you in over a month. I understand you not wanting to come to the house and shit, but even when I try to meet you somewhere out on the town, you shut me out. I'm losing it, Mami. What do you need?"

Carlos was trying to be patient with Bliss, but she was drifting away from everybody. He was at a loss of what to do. He wanted to respect her space and healing process, but he was hurting and needed to be close to his daughter. It hurt him further to know that she didn't want to be around him. He carried the burden of what happened to her. There was not a day that he didn't think about it.

"You know what? Just enjoy your birthday, baby girl. Don't forget to bring something to the cookout on Sunday. So go out and have some fun, get some rest tomorrow, and I'll see you Sunday. Love you."

Bliss was about to respond, but the phone went dead. Sighing deeply, she stood up and made her way into the kitchen. She went to the freezer and grabbed her bottle of Peach Cîroc and poured herself a shot.

"Uh-uh, bitch, I know ya triflin ass not taking birthday shots without me." Letty said, sashaying into the kitchen. She looked good in a powder pink mid-drift tank top, black leather leggings, and a pair of powder pink pumps. She rocked some black accessories, and her hair was slicked back into a high bun, with Chinese bangs.

"Of course not," Bliss said, while trying not to laugh. She failed and Letty rolled her eyes.

"You never were a good liar. It's against the code of ethics to take shots by yourself on ya birthday."

Blissed laughed at Letty as she poured another shot. "Well, I'm sorry for almost breaking the code."

"Don't let that shit happen again, bitch." They clinked glasses and downed the shot. Letty leaned over and gave Bliss a kiss on the cheek. "Happy birthday, Esa."

Letty's phoned dinged with a notification. After checking her phone, she looked at Bliss and said, "Come on let's go; Riq downstairs."

Taking another shot for the road and a couple of selfies, Bliss and Letty gathered their items and headed to meet Tyriq outside.

On the ride over Bliss laughed to herself as she watched Riq and Letty perform "This Could Be Us" by Rae Sremmurd as if they were in concert.

*"Girl, improvise, look me in my eyes and lie to me. Lie to me, act like I'll believe anything."*

She sat up and joined them as the chorus came on.

*"This could be us but you're playing (money make the world go 'round)*
*I'm high, I hope I don't sound crazy (money make ya girl go down)"*

Being high and tipsy, Bliss was in her own zone. She pushed all of her thoughts to the back of her mind and focused on having a good time.

Arriving at the Club, Tyriq gave the keys to the valet and walked around the car to meet the girls. Bliss and Letty each wrapped around one of Tyriq's extended arms as they waltzed past the line of onlookers and headed towards the club's entrance.

"What's up, Big Black?" Riq greeted the bouncer while dapping him up.

"What's up, Riq? Ladies?" He nodded at Bliss and Letty, his eyes lingering on Bliss.

"You know my girl, Letty, but this my little sister, Bliss."

"Nice to meet you," Bliss said while smiling politely.

"The pleasure is all mine." Big Black continued to look Bliss up and down.

"Stop staring at my sister like I'm not right here nigga," Tyriq said. "The crew coming through tonight if they not already in there."

"Aw, shit. Don't start no shit tonight, Riq, and don't tear nothing up; just call me, and I'll handle whatever."

Riq smirked, "I'm always on my best behavior, yo." With that, he led the ladies inside of the club.

Crossing the threshold of the VIP section, Bliss got the surprise of her life when she heard, "Happy birthday, Esa!!" being yelled. She covered her mouth in awe as multiple flashes went off catching this moment.

There were quite a few people there to help bring in Esa's birthday. The majority were people that she met through Tyriq. There were also some that she and Letty knew from high school.

Esa went around and said hey to everybody and showed appreciation as they blessed her with money and cards, which contained more money, the she made her way to the couch that Letty and Riq were perched on.

Letty threw her arms around Esa's shoulders before giving her a kiss on the cheek. "Happy birthday, Esabella."

"Thank you, Letty," Esa said smiling at her best friend before hugging her.

"Aye, I'm the nigga paying for this, where my love at?" Tyriq said, plopping down in-between the girls.

Bliss gave him a hug, "Thank you, big brother,".

"You already know, Es." he said kissing her on the forehead.

Letty ordered a round of shots, while Tyriq stood up on the couch.

"Yo! Everybody gather 'round! Hear ye' mufuckas!" Tyriq yelled over the music. "I just wanna thank you all before I get too fucked up. Cause a nigga will forget. But anyway, thank you for helping Letty pull off this surprise gathering for baby sis. We 'preciate you niggas; now turn the fuck up! Happy birthday, Esa!" he finished, raising his shot in the air.

"Happy birthday Esa!" Everybody repeated before downing their shots of liquor.

*****

After her fifth dance, Bliss began to walk back to her seat. She rolled her eyes as Letty followed behind her and asked her for the fifteenth millionth time, "You sure you good, Esa?"

"I told you I'm fine, Let." She said tersely.

"There's no reason for you to have an attitude, Bliss. I'm just checking on you."

"If I told you that I'm fine, then stop asking me, Letty. I'm tryna have a good time, but that's becoming increasingly harder with you breathing down my neck." Bliss poured her a shot and downed it quickly before walking away from Letty and towards the double doors that led to the outside patio.

Letty was hot on her heels, "If you want some space, that's all you have to say."

"I don't know how many times I have to tell you that. Or how many different ways you want me to say it, but back off, Letty. I'm fine; I'm actually having an amazing time. The only thing that's ruining it is constantly being reminded that there's something to be worried about. You dragged me out of the house to have a good time. So let me have it." Bliss stood and walked towards the patio door.

"Don't be gone too long, Esa!" Letty yelled after her. "We still gotta meet Riq's friend."

Ignoring her, Bliss walked back inside.

Downstairs on the dance floor, Bliss was dancing with a random that couldn't even keep up, when she felt herself being flown forward.

"Oh, shit!" she heard a stranger yell over the music, before she felt a pair of strong arms reach out and grab her. She was rendered speechless by the jolt that he caused to travel through her body. She turned around to look at who knocked her over and was stunned silent by the most mesmerizing dark brown gaze that she has ever witnessed.

Mentally clearing her head, she spoke up. "Next time, watch where you're going."

Squeezing her waist a little tighter, the tall stranger leaned forward until his lips barely brushed against her ear. Her breath caught as his deep and sexy baritone graced her ear drums, "I couldn't hear you, Ma. You mind repeating it for me?"

A chill rippled through her body, and goose bumps formed on her arms causing her to shiver against the handsome stranger. She was intoxicated by the scent of his Polo cologne.

Bliss wrapped her arms around his neck and gently tugged him down until his ear was leveled to her mouth. She had the urge to bite his earlobe, but instead, she said, "I said watch where you going next time. You stepped on my toes."

He pulled back and looked at her face before he fell out in laughter. She didn't understand what was so funny, because she was dead ass serious. He smiled before placing his lips by her ear again. The soft stubble from his beard tickled as his lips moved.

"I'm sorry, shorty; it won't happen again." he said.

"It better not or you paying for my next pedicure."

He chuckled deeply in her ear before responding, "You got it, Ma."

She rolled her eyes, "My name ain't Ma." she said before removing herself from the hold that he had on her mentally and physically. Stepping away, she turned and tried to walk away. He gently grabbed her arm, stopping her mid-step. Stepping up behind her, he let go of her arm and placed his hands on her waist. This man had trouble written all over him.

"Where you going?" he asked her.

"I'm sure I'll see you around."

He turned her around to face him, "Can I at least get ya name beautiful?"

"I'm Esa. And you?"

"I'm Bent. So check this, Miss Esa. I'm not quite ready to let you go yet. You mind having one dance with me?"

"Just was waiting for you to ask me" she smirked.

Bliss had never interacted with a man like this, except for Junior, but she knew him for a while, so she didn't count that as out of the ordinary. With Bent, she was sarcastic and flirty, and it all came naturally.

Bent didn't miss a beat as he gently grabbed her hand and turned her around just as "Liquor", by Chris Brown, bumped over the club's speakers. Bliss started to slowly whine her hips as she let the smooth beat take over her senses, and she left all thoughts and worries to the side, as she went off of instinct.

After a few seconds, she felt Bent step up behind her and fall in step with her movements. It was as if they were in their own little world. Esa turned around to face him, as she swayed to the music.

When they locked eyes, Bliss got lost in his chocolate orbs. Bent stepped closer to her as he wrapped his arms back around her waist, stopping right above her plump ass. Their eyes stayed locked as they tried to become one on the dance floor.

Bliss was baffled yet captivated by the hold he had on her. She told herself to just keep it moving, but her feet stayed planted. She wanted to know more about him. She couldn't place it, but she knew she didn't want to say good night.

"Es! Let's go; I've been looking for you, yo." Before Bliss could react, Letty snatched her arm and started to drag her away. Letty didn't stop until they were half way on the other side of the club, near the VIP entrance.

"Have you lost your mind?! I've been looking for you for the last half hour." Letty pulled Bliss up the stairs and down a dimly lit hallway.

Bliss snatched her arm away, "You're the one that's lost their mind. Don't grab me like that, Letty. I'm not playing with you. Go chill out, cause you really pissing me off." Bliss stormed off in the opposite direction from where they were heading.

"Esa! Will you slow down? I'm tryna talk to you! You had me scared I was looking all over for you I didn't know what happened to you."

"Leave me alone, Letty! I'm not fucking twelve a'ight? I can handle myself." Bliss saw a silhouette walking towards them, but she couldn't make out who it was.

"Well, how's that working out for you so far, huh? Last time I checked, your self-preservation skills weren't on one hundred." Esa stopped mid stride and turned to look at Letty in disbelief. Letty instantly regretted what she said, "Shit, Es. I'm, I'm sorry," she slurred.

"Fuck you, Let." When Bliss turned back around, she was face to face with Bent. She smiled a little despite her blood boiling. She stepped closer to him and pulled him down so she could whisper in his ear, "Can you get me out of here?"

He smirked down at her, "Just was waiting for you to ask me."

Bliss smiled shyly before quickly leading the way back to the table to get her clutch. She had set it down when she stepped away from Letty earlier. After Bliss had her belongings, Bent grabbed her hand and led them down the stairs towards the exit.

"I'll see you later OG." Bent said to Big Black, who was now sitting at the bar flirting with the female bartender.

"I see you, Bent!" Big Black said, excitedly, when he noticed Bentley holding hands with Bliss.

Bent chuckled, "Yo ass crazy. I'll holla at you later."

"A'ight, youngin, be safe out here."

When they got outside, Bent's Range Rover was already waiting for them. Bent walked them to the truck and opened the door for Bliss. "Hop in," he smiled at her. She smiled back, and with his help, she successfully got situated in the truck. "Where to, Miss Esa?"

"Anywhere."

"'Nough said."

# Chapter Six

Bliss sat back in her seat as Bentley swerved through traffic. She was beginning to rethink her decision.

Maybe Letty was right. Maybe she didn't have any self-preservation skills, but she was tired of living scared.

She wanted to have fun and not feel ashamed of it. She couldn't explain it, but she got a good vibe from Bent. She felt comfortable leaving with him. She just prayed it wasn't a mistake.

"You down to ride or you want me to drop you off somewhere?" Bent's voice broke through her thoughts. She looked over at him confused. "I'm just asking. You look like you over there re-contemplating your life decisions." he chuckled.

She cracked a smile, "Nah, just vibing."

"A'ight, Miss Esa. Just say the word; the ball in ya court."

"I'm riding with you." She looked over at him, as he nodded and turned the music up.

Bliss sat up straight in her seat when she felt the car come to a complete stop. She wiped her eyes in an attempt to shake the sleep away. She looked out the window to get a better picture of where they were and noticed that they were at Coney Island, one of the local beaches and amusement parks.

"Come on, Miss Esa," Bent said hopping out of the truck. He walked around to open her door. After helping her out of the truck, he got a blanket out of the backseat.

"You hungry?" he asked her as they approached *Nathan's Famous,* a staple food joint in Brooklyn.

"Hell, yeah. I swear I could eat more than two Rasputia's combined right now." she said seriously causing Bent to burst out in laughter. She furrowed her eyebrows, "What's so funny?"

"You." he smirked down at her before shaking his head.

They ordered their food and drinks and walked further down past the boardwalk onto the beach. There were a few people out, but it was nearing one am, so the crowd was getting sparse.

"You smoke?" Bent asked lighting up a blunt.

"You can't tell?" she giggled. "I know I got the raccoon eyes going on."

"I just thought you was tired." He passed her the blunt.

"You're sweet." she said blowing the smoke out and smiling.

They became quiet as they shared the blunt and listened to the waves crashing against the shore. Bliss loved when she could be quiet around someone and it not be an awkward silence. Sometimes, she didn't have much to say; she just observed and enjoyed being in the moment.

Bent wrapped his arms around Bliss' waist from behind as they stood at the shore and let the mild waves crash against their feet. He bent down and placed a kiss softly against her neck.

She shuddered as the currents he caused traveled through her body.

Feeling her shiver, Bentley rubbed his hands up and down her bare arms to warm her up.

She giggled before turning around in his arms, looking up at him.

Their eyes locked, and Bliss could feel her heart rate speed up. The energy between them was palpitating. She was mesmerized as she watched as his tongue peeked out to wet his lips.

Grabbing her face with his hand, Bent kissed her forehead. Bliss' breath caught as the chills ran up and down her spine. What was it about this dude that had her feeling like this? It was as if he had her underneath a spell.

This man was the epitome of sexy. The way his crinkly dreads hung loosely had Bliss' knees wobbling a little bit.

She closed her eyes as Bent lowered his head towards hers. His scent surrounded her as he closed the distance that was left between them.

"Can I kiss you, Miss Esa?" He kissed her once. Gently, yet firm.

"That, you don't have to ask." she said, before he covered her mouth with his completely.

The sensations that shot through her body caught Esa by surprise. A wave of warmth and heat flashed throughout her body as she kissed him back. Her stomach fluttered so hard that she thought it was going to jump out and fall into the sand.

Bentley gently bit her bottom lip, causing the floodgates to open and her thong to become soaked. Moaning softly, she slid her arms around his neck.

He left a trail of fire across Bliss' thigh, as he slid his large hands through her high slit skirt and palmed her soft ass. His touch was gentle as he gripped her ass tighter and pulled her closer.

Bliss pulled away reluctantly when her lungs began to scream at her for air.

Bentley moved one hand to the back of her head before scratching his nails against her scalp. He pulled her head back before attacking her lips with his again. He gripped her ass tighter as she snaked her tongue around his.

Sucking on her bottom lip, Bent gave her one last peck before pulling away. "Come on, Esa." He turned and began the walk back to the truck.

"Where we going?" she asked following behind him.

"To the crib." He stopped walking and turned to look at her. "That cool?"

She thought it over for a minute before nodding. "Don't be trying nothing either, Bent." She smiled.

"I ain't gotta try, Miss Esa. What I want, I get." he said nonchalantly before kissing her forehead. "I ain't tryna fuck you yet, though. I'm just not tryna say goodnight to you.

When I'm tryna fuck, you'll know." He kissed her before grabbing her hand and making their way back to the truck.

Bent guided his Range into the basement parking deck of a building. Getting out of the truck, he walked to open Bliss' door for her. Grabbing her hand, he helped her down and out of the truck. Once she was on the ground, he looked at her weirdly.

"Why you looking at me like that?" Her eyebrows furrowed over her hazel eyes.

"Yo little ass shorter than I thought." Bent said while smiling. He fell out in laughter when she punched him in his chest.

"I took my heels off, ass. Shit, my feet were hurting." she said, laughing, while hitting him again for fun. Before she registered what was going on, Bliss was lifted in the air and sitting back in her seat with her legs dangling out of the car. "What are you doing?"

He turned around so his back was facing Bliss before kneeling down in front of her. Catching on, she placed her arms gently around his shoulder and wrapped her legs around his waist. Once he stood up to his full height, Bliss tightened her hold around him.

He wrapped his arms around her legs before walking them to an elevator, which opened immediately allowing them access. "So how tall are you anyway shorty?"

She smacked her teeth, "My name ain't shorty, either, so I hope you got a different pet name."

"Oh, word? That's how you feel?" He looked over his shoulder at her; she nodded while smiling. "Touché, Miss Esa, forgive me." He laughed.

"All is forgiven." she giggled.

The elevator doors opened, and Bentley walked them to the second out of the two doors on the floor. He unlocked the door, turned on the lights, and carried her straight into the kitchen. Sitting her down on the island, he turned around, in-between her legs, to face her.

Bentley tightened his grip on her waist and stepped closer to her. This girl was doing something to him, and he couldn't even begin to explain what it was. Every coherent thought he had went out the window whenever he looked at her. He felt like he couldn't control his movements; he was moving off of instinct.

Not being able to think straight, he asked the first question that popped into his head. "You hungry?"

She shook her head slowly, *"Not for food, anyway,"* she thought to herself.

Somehow, her hands found their way to the back of his neck where she began playing with a single dread; gently twisting it with her fingers.

Her clit ached as his plump, soft lips met hers. Every nerve in her body jumped alive as she felt his tongue tickling her bottom lip, begging for entrance. Bliss moaned softly as their tongues battled for dominance. Relaxing fully, she let him have control.

Ending the kiss, Bent grabbed a handful of ass and pulled her closer to him. He left a trail of kisses against her neck and down her collar bone.

"I gotta pee," Esa giggled, her low eyes crinkling with laugh lines. "Whenever I drink, I swear my bladder turns into the size of a pea."

Bentley fell out laughing, "You mad silly."

"I'm so serious," she giggled.

He kissed her one last time before helping her off of the counter. He turned and started walking down the hallway towards his room. Turning on the lights as he went alone, he led her to the guest bathroom.

"I'mma be down the hall if you need me." Bent said, leaving her to use the restroom.

"Hey Bent?" she called after him.

"Wassup?"

"Do you have something I can change into? Like some shorts or something?"

"I think you a little too small for my stuff, Esa." he said laughing.

"Come on, Bent, I know you got something. I wanna be comfortable, and I can't do that in a barely there skirt."

"You the one that put that shit on," Bent laughed.

"So? I'm not hearing no complaints from you, so I guess it served a good purpose."

"You never were hearing any from me to begin with. I love the skirt, Ma. Dead ass. That shit is fucking sexy."

She blushed and looked away, "Thank you."

"I got you, though, hold on." He disappeared up the hall only to return shortly with a small pile of clothes. "Here," he handed her the clothes. "I'll be in the living room."

"Thank you."

"Bet."

Bent brought her a pair of black Polo cuffed sweatpants, and a gray V-neck t-shirt. The pants were big, but luckily, there was a drawstring, so whatever space her hips and ass didn't take up, she could tighten the rest.

"You good?" Bent asked once Esa joined him in the living room.

"Yeah, I'm good. I feel so much better. Thanks." She found him on the couch where he was watching ESPN and smoking a blunt. He was dressed down in a pair of black basketball shorts and a wife beater. His toned, tattooed arms were on full display, enticing Bliss to bite them.

Straddling his lap, she took the blunt from him and brought it to her lips. She French inhaled as she watched him watch her. Biting her lip, she looked away.

He turned her head back towards him before slowly bringing his head to hers. The kiss he gave her set her whole being on fire.

When he broke apart from her, Bliss snaked her hand into his head as her fingers found a dread to twist.

"I never got to finish my dance," Bent said causing Bliss to furrow her brows. She watched as he muted the T.V. and pressed on a small remote control.

"What?" she giggled. Her high was settling in, making everything funny and hazy.

Her body was so sensitive to touch that every time his warm breath blew against her skin, her clit jumped.

"You owe me a dance." he smiled as the music started to play in the background.

"How you figure?"

Without answering her, Bent stood up while holding Bliss and started to sway to the melodic beat. His hands made their way to her plump ass and squeezed.

Bliss giggled, "I take it you're an ass man?"

Bent chortled, "I guess you can say that. I like it all. If I can squeeze it, I like it." He squeezed her love handles for emphasis. She fell out laughing before reaching up for a kiss.

Bent moved them over to the wall and placed Bliss up against it. He tongued her down causing her pussy to drip and her nipples to ache as lust coursed through her veins. The want that she had for this man was like nothing that she'd ever experienced before. She bit his lip causing him to hiss with pleasure. Kissing her a final time, he pulled away to look at her, "you better stop Miss Esa."

"Stop what?" she asked looking up at him.

"You know what you doing. I'm tryna be on my best behavior right now, and you making it hard on a nigga."

"I can feel that," she giggled, as she reached down and massaged his growing hard-on through his shorts. Her mouth watered when she felt how big he was already.

"Nah, you aint feel it yet." he said. "You bout to if you don't cut it out."

While maintaining eye contact with Bentley, she grabbed one of his hands and slipped it down her pants. Her eyes rolled back as his fingers ghosted over her swollen clit, sending chills up her spine.

She pulled his hand back and two of his fingers were coated in her essence, then she slipped one into her mouth before sticking the other one in his.

She slowly swirled her tongue around his finger, moaning as she savored the taste.

"This the last time I'mma ask you. You sure this what you want?"

Ignoring him, Bliss placed his other finger in her mouth and began sucking on them gently. She took his hand and placed them back down her pants onto her hot waiting center.

Bliss gasped loudly as Bent entered his two lubricated fingers inside of her. Moving in and out slowly, Bent kissed Bliss roughly before placing his mouth by her ear. "This pussy feels so good." He bit her earlobe, "You gone get that shit wet for me?"

She moaned as he picked his pace up. He circled her sensitive nub while simultaneously fucking her with his wide fingers. He grinned when he found her spot, and she started moaning and fucking his hand back. "That's it; make it juicy for me."

Without warning, he snatched Bliss' pants off and lifted her above his head and against the wall. Then, he moved her thong to the side and dived in, giving long, slow strokes to her bundle of nerves while relentlessly circling it with his wet and warm tongue. He didn't let up until she latched onto his dreads for dear life and started screaming his name.

"Ohhhh, Bent." Her body tensed up as her first orgasm washed over her. "Mmm, oh my God." she moaned before biting her bottom lip.

"Mhm," he hummed as he lapped up her sweet nectar. Her honey to him was like blood to a vampire. One drop, and he was done.

There was no way he would allow her to ever fuck anybody else but him from here on out. Once she let him get a taste, she sealed her fate. "I see you, Miss Esa," he smirked. "I'm 'bout to have fun with yo little ass."

He let her body slide down his as he licked his way up hers. Bentley paused his trail to rip her shirt over her head before paying attention to her budded, chocolate mounds.

"Oh, shit," she moaned, as he pressed both of her breasts together and flicked his tongue across her sensitive nipples at once.

Once Bentley halted his pleasurable attack on her nipples. He covered her mouth with his own in a heated kiss. She moaned at the taste of her-self on his lips and tongue. Her hands found their way into his hair as he caused her body to catch on fire.

Bliss' breath caught in her throat, and her moans silenced as Bentley filled and deliciously stretched her to capacity. Cumming instantly on his massive size, Bliss closed her eyes as the euphoric feeling washed over her. Bentley let her get adjusted to his thick 10 inches before slowly moving in and out of her. Kissing her, he asked, "You okay, baby?"

Not being able to speak, Bliss just nodded her head as several moans slipped out. She had never felt such pleasure before in her life.

"Ohhhh fuck, Bent." she moaned loudly, finding her voice.

Her pussy was so tight and wet that Bent couldn't blink too hard or he was gonna bust. "Got damn this pussy so fucking good." He bit down on her shoulder, causing her walls to squeeze around him impossibly tighter, as she exploded. "Fuck, Esa. Squeeze that dick, Ma. Shit." She was cumming so hard that she damn near pushed him out.

She pushed her hand against his arm signaling that she wanted him to put her leg down; he ignored her and picked up the pace of his strokes. Placing his mouth next to her ear, he bit down before licking over it to soothe the sting.

"Take this dick, Ma. I want you to make that pussy come one more time, Juicy. Can you do that for me?" he said in her ear. When she didn't respond, he stopped his strokes and pulled back to look at her.

"Why'd you stop?" She whined. When he wouldn't move, she tried to grind her hips down to feel the wonderful friction that he provided. He held her thighs tighter and pulled out, only leaving the tip in. "Bent, quit playing." He was torturing her.

"Answer my question, and I'll give you what you want." He kissed her. "You gone make that pussy come for me again?" She sucked in a sharp gasp as he slammed all the way into her. He pulled out again leaving just the tip in. "I can't hear you."

She scratched her nails down his back, causing him to shudder and slam into her repeatedly.

"Ohhhh fuck, Bent." she moaned loudly as her body began convulsing uncontrollably.

"Mhm, that's what I'm talking about, Esa. Make that shit spray. Got damn." He sped his pace up chasing that tingle up his spine. "Fuck!" he yelled as his nut came full force.

They stood there for a minute, each lost in their own post-coital thoughts, trying to get their bearings together.

Once he gained the strength, Bent carried Bliss to the master bathroom where he ran a shower for her. He planned on letting her have her time, but she pulled him in the shower with her.

What was supposed to be a quick shower ended up being forty-five minutes long with Bent fucking Bliss against the shower tile. The water had long turned cold by the time they got out.

After getting dressed, they returned to the living room where they set up camp on Bent's sectional. She braided her hair back into two braids before getting comfortable.

Bliss was having a good time as they smoked, ate, watched TV and played the game. They talked about everything from their favorite artist to zombie apocalypses. They argued over everything from sports to which Denzel Washington movie was the best.

Falling asleep to Bentley running his fingers through her hair and rubbing her back, Bliss slept calmly. She rarely had a night to where she didn't have a nightmare, but tonight was one of those rare times.

*****

The sound of her phone vibrating woke Bliss up from her slumber. Sitting up, she yawned before taking in her surroundings. She was no longer in the living room on the couch that she fell asleep on.

Instead, she was in a darkened room, laying in a very big bed. She stretched before throwing the comforter back and reaching for her phone that was sitting on the table next to her.

She had a list of missed calls and text messages from Letty, her dad, and Junior. Even Tyriq's name popped up a few times. She checked the last missed call and saw that it was Junior.

Pushing his name, she settled back into the pillows as she waited for the call to connect.

"About time you answered your damn phone. Where the fuck you been at Esa? I've been calling you all night."

"Hey to you, too, Junior."

"Man, I ain't tryna hear that smart shit right now, Esa. Where you at?"

"I'm at a friend's house. I'm good, so you can stop worrying."

"What's the address, Bliss? I'm 'bout to come and get you."

"You back home?" Bliss perked up at the news.

"Fuck you mean? Of course, I'm home. Letty calling me all fucking night talking about she couldn't find your ass so what you expect me to do? That shit not cool, Bliss."

"My phone died; I-" Bliss started.

"What's the address? I'm not tryna hear that extra shit man."

Bliss was taken aback by the way Junior was talking to her. "You don't have to talk to me like that Junior."

"Look, if you not tryna give me the address, meet me at the crib in an hour. I ain't playing, Bliss. You don't want me to come and find ya ass."

The call ended, and Bliss sighed deeply. She didn't feel like dealing with this shit.

She heard what sounded like the front door, so she got out of the bed and fixed herself up before padding her way into the living room. She watched as the front door opened and

Bentley waltzed himself in to the house bearing a couple of bags. He put the bags down on the island in the kitchen.

"Good morning, Miss Esa." He kissed her before tossing his wallet on the kitchen counter. It bounced off and hit the floor.

"Good morning," she blushed.

Smiling at her, Bent turned around and walked down the hallway towards his room. "I'll be back."

"Ok."

Bliss bent over to pick his wallet up when she noticed that a couple of papers fell out. Opening his wallet, she began to put the papers back in there., when her eyes landed on a folded piece of paper.

Something told her to open up the small square. Following her instincts, she picked the small piece of paper up.

Unfolding it, she revealed that it was a sonogram picture. Tears sprang to her eyes as she scanned over the picture several times just to make sure she was seeing everything correctly.

Her heart was telling her that this was Cielo that she was looking at. She hadn't seen the picture since the day that she lost her baby.

She confirmed her suspicions when she glanced at the top corner of the picture and saw her name.

Her heart pounded in her chest as a million questions barraged her mind at once. She was so confused as to why he had it in the first place.

"What the fuck are you doing?" Before she knew it, she was being flown backwards by her neck. Her back slammed against a wall, causing her breath to get caught in her throat. "You tryna steal from me, bitch?!"

Opening her eyes, she witnessed Bent standing over her with a menacing look on his face. His hand was around her throat as he held her against the wall.

"Pl...ease," she tried talking, but he had a death grip on her neck. She grabbed at his hands and tried to pry them off. "I-I," He squeezed tighter making her words cease.

"Just get the fuck outta my house, yo." Bentley released Bliss from the death grip that he had on her neck.

Bliss bent over trying to help the oxygen move through her body. Her throat was on fire and her chest cried out in pain. Her blood boiled throughout her body as rage coursed through her veins.

"I aint got all day; get the fuck out." Bent pushed her towards the door.

Bliss stood up straight, cocked her arm all the way back, and punched him in the face. He stumbled backwards providing her with the room to run towards the door.

He ran after her as she ran towards the front door. He caught up to her by the entrance to the kitchen and snatched her up by her collar.

Bliss saw something out of the corner of her eye and grabbed it off of the counter. She smashed the glass against his forehead with all the strength that she could muster up.

"Arrrgh!" Bent grabbed his forehead as he began to bleed profusely.

Bliss ran out of his apartment and down the stairs that lead to the outside world. She didn't have any shoes so she lifted a pair of flip flops from one of the outside displays of a store.

She made sure she was more than a few blocks away before ducking into a McDonalds. She took a seat at a table that was away from the door, but provided her with a view of the windows and the door so she could watch who was coming in and out.

Pulling out her phone, she called Junior.

"You got fifteen minutes," he answered on the first ring.

"I need you to come and get me June. I'm at the Mickeys on Atlantic and Vanderbilt." Bliss rasped out.

"Be there in ten." He said before the call disconnected.

Bliss hung her head low; what the fuck did she get herself into? Her mind was spinning as she couldn't wrap her mind around one single thought.

Her emotions were all over the place as she thought about what had just happened.

She had just had the best mind blowing sex with someone that literally swept her off of her feet. In a club of all places.

It was like, around Bent, all rational thoughts went out of the window. He had a pull on her that tugged at a deeper place that she had no idea even existed.

She wanted to jump on him and fuck the shit out of him. In the same breath, she wanted to shoot him in the kneecap.

She felt stupid for liking him and even allowing herself to go as far as she did.

*"What is it about me that attracts these types of bum ass niggas?"* she thought as she looked up and saw a few people staring at her like she was crazy.

"Can I help you?!" she asked them. One woman rolled her eyes and looked away, while the others dropped their heads into their phones.

She couldn't blame them though. She was pretty sure that she had a bruise on her neck, her clothes were too big, and her hair was coming out of her braids so she had random hairs sticking up everywhere.

On top of that, her size 'D' cup breasts were free-balling and swinging in the wind because her bra was at Bent's house. She took it off last night and didn't have a chance to put it back on this morning.

Looking out of the window, she watched as Junior's car pulled into the parking lot. She was outside before he could put the car in park. Hopping in, she sat back silently. Junior grabbed her face gently and turned her head to look at him. She looked up and met his concerned stare.

"I'mma ask this question as calmly as I can." He paused and took a deep breath. "What happened to your neck, Bliss?"

Her gaze fell from his as she shook her head gently. She just wanted a hot shower, a blunt, some tea, and to be in Junior's bed cuddled up under him watching *Rent* on his flat screen.

Not getting the answer he wanted, Junior let her face go and turned his attention to the road. Sighing deeply, Bliss turned in her seat and watched as the city whizzed by.

# Chapter Seven

Bliss walked into Junior's room after getting out of the shower. He was sitting on the edge of his bed smoking a blunt.

She walked over to his drawer and pulled out one of his t-shirts. He held the blunt out with one hand while patting the spot next to him.

"You owe me some answers."

Taking a deep breath, Bliss joined him. Her eyes traveled up his body as she drunk him in. Junior was beautiful. His golden brown arms were covered in tattoos that Bliss just wanted to lick. His neatly trimmed beard gave him that grown man sexy and surrounded his soft, desirable lips.

His light brown eyes were framed by his naturally thick, arched eyebrows and his curly eyelashes that Bliss was always jealous of. His 6'0 even height was matched perfectly with his broad shoulders and basketball player build.

Bliss would be a liar if she said that she wasn't attracted to Junior. They just had this connection that she couldn't explain. It was like her day was not complete unless she saw him. He knew just what to say and he understood her without having to try.

They mesh so well that Bliss wished that she would have met him years ago; she would've paid attention to him.

Her thoughts flashed over to Bent, and she quickly pushed it to the back of her mind. She would just have to get over what little feelings she did have. They're not even together, and she already got a bruise and a sore body. *"I'll pass"*. She thought as she sat with her knees to her chest and squished her toes between Junior's thigh and the bed.

She looked over at Junior and smiled a little. She hated that he cut his trip short for her, but she was ecstatic that he was home, and she felt whole again. Like she could breathe.

"Stop eye fucking me, Esa, before you start something that I know yo sexy ass ain't ready for." Junior said, seriously, while handing her the blunt.

She grinned before taking a pull. "Fuck outta here, June."

"A'ight, I hear you, Es." He ran his hand through her hair. "I'm glad you washed this shit; I missed ya curls."

"I know. You kept bitching about it." She rolled her eyes playfully.

"Watch ya mouth," he laughed. "So what happened yesterday, Es?"

She recounted the part about the wallet and what transpired after that. Junior was quiet as she told him what happened but he was burning hot. He just didn't want to cut her off.

He knew that she would shut down if he started to yell right now. He had to know all of what happened, so he would know how many bullets to put in the muthafucka that did this.

94

"What's his name?" he asked laying back on the bed, looking up at the ceiling.

Bliss was quiet as she continued to smoke the blunt. She wasn't going to give Bent's name up. She knew Junior well and knew that he would find this nigga and kill him. He had way too many guns for her to try and hide them all.

Even though it was fucked up what Bent did, Bliss didn't want him dead. Shit, she still had questions that only he had the answers to.

"You too quiet for me, Esa. What's the nigga name?"

"I'm not telling you Junior."

He sat straight up and looked at her. "Fuck you mean?"

"Exactly what I said. I'm not telling you." She blew out a breath, she hated arguing, and this was about to become an argument. She pulled on the blunt long and hard before passing it to him. She French inhaled as she waited for his response.

"I'm not understanding why not, Esa."

"I got my own shit that I gotta handle first, and I need him alive for that. If I give you his name, it's a wrap, so I need you to just leave it alone, Junior. A'ight?"

He smacked his teeth, "You dead ass?"

"Yes, Junior."

Junior was quiet as he laid back down. What Bliss was asking of him right now was hard as fuck, but she seemed adamant about it so he would let it go for right now.

"A'ight, man," Junior reluctantly agreed. Sitting up, he grabbed the blunt from her and took the last few pulls before putting the roach in the ashtray.

"Promise me." Bliss stuck her pinky out.

Junior smacked his teeth, "I said a'ight. My word is my bond."

Bliss didn't waver as she held her pinky in place. Sighing dejectedly, Junior locked his pinky with hers before they both kissed their fists.

Bliss leaned over and kissed his cheek. "I'll make it up to you."

Junior grabbed her face in between his hands and kissed her softly on her lips. Bliss felt a warmth spread throughout her body as she relaxed against him. Giving her a few more pecks on her soft, pillow top lips, Junior forced himself to pull away.

"Put some clothes on before you get fucked, guh."

Bliss blushed as she giggled. She knew he was serious, so she went back to the guest room where she had her clothes laid out and got dressed.

*****

Junior parked his slate gray Lexus in front of Carlos' brownstone as Bliss popped a piece of gum in her mouth, put on some Chapstick, and sprayed some of her perfume. They had smoked on the ride over, and Bliss didn't want to smell like a pound of loud; she had to keep it cute.

She checked Junior out as he finished off the drink that she made him before they left his house.

He looked good in his customized *'Damn Gina'* white tank top. The words were written in the same font and colors as the *Martin* TV show logo. He rocked some black cargo shorts and a pair of all white Air Max 90's. Topping off his look, he rocked a white and black Brooklyn Nets snapback.

His half sleeved tattooed arms were oiled down and on full display. It took everything in her not to lick all over his sexy tattoos. The way they glistened against his smooth peanut butter complexioned skin beckoned Bliss. She shook her head clear from the direction that her thoughts were going before giving herself a once over in the mirror.

Matching his fly, Bliss had on a black and white *Crooklyn* baseball jersey, ripped distressed cutoff shorts, and a pair of black, white, and red Air Jordan 13's. She kept it simple by adding a pair of big gold hoops and letting a few matching gold bangles dangle from her wrist.

After grabbing the macaroni and cheese, some sodas, and the ice out of the backseat, Bliss and Junior made their way into the house. After dropping the items off in the kitchen, they proceeded to the backyard through the sliding glass door.

Bliss smiled as she took in the scene before her. The music was bumping some oldies as her dad manned the grill. Her sister was sitting at the card table playing spades with her husband Lucky and a couple of their dad's friends.

Sinaya, or Sin, as the family called her, was Bliss' older sister, she was twenty-two and had a five-year-old son named Angel. Sin and her husband had been married for 4 years but they've been together for 6 years.

Bliss and Sin looked identical except that Sin was a bit chunkier around the hips, butt, and stomach. Sinaya's eyes were a deep brown like their mother's, whereas Bliss had hazel eyes like their father. Other than that, you would think that they were twins, and people would often mistake them for each other all the time.

"Aye, look who decided to come out of hiding!" Sinaya said, as Bliss and Junior walked into the small backyard.

Bliss laughed as she hugged her older sister. "Good to see you, Mami. Where's Ti-Ti's baby?"

"He's playing with the neighborhood kids. Who knows where they at." Sin said, plopping back into her seat. "Hey Junior; it's good to see you out from behind that sandwich counter."

"Good to see you too, Ma." He shook his head before dapping Lucky up. Sin always said the wildest shit.

Bliss walked over to her dad after making her rounds and saying hello to everyone. Kissing him on the cheek she said "Hola, Daddy."

"Hey, baby girl," he said, swiping at the smoke coming from the grill with his barbecue fork. "Glad that you could make it."

"Of course, Daddy." She kissed him on the cheek.

"How was your birthday?" He flipped the chicken breast over.

Bliss rolled her eyes, "I don't wanna talk about it right now."

"Respect." Closing the lid to the grill, he looked over at her for the first time. His eyes bulged out of his head as he took in her neck. "What the fuck happened?! I swear, I'mma kill him, Bliss." He examined her neck tenderly.

Sin perked up from the card table, "How you even know it was Mario, Daddy?"

Lucky looked up from his cards and looked at Sinaya with a frown, "Sin, sit yo ass down and get out they business."

"That's my sister, so it is my business," she rolled her eyes before taking a sip of her Corona.

"I'm not gone say it again." He cut her eyes at her making her finally take heed and have a seat.

Bliss gave her sister the side eye, but chose to ignore her further. "Daddy, I'll tell you later. It's not really the time right now."

"I'mma hold you to that, Esa. Fa real."

"A'ight, Daddy I hear you."

"Hello, everybody!" Letty said, making herself known as she walked into the back yard. She made her rounds and kissed Bliss on the cheek.

Being annoyed with one another, they still weren't speaking, but they always greeted each other and showed love.

It was a ground rule and a reason why they had been friends for so long.

"Where's Riq?"

"He said he had to make a stop real quick. He should be here any minute."

As if on cue, Tyriq waltzed through the back door. "Dun da da dun da da; the champ is here!" he sang, trying to sound like Jay-Z. "What's good, yo?" he greeted everyone before making his rounds.

"I'll be back," Bliss said to her father. She wanted to find her nephew before it got too late. He nodded his understanding.

Bliss walked up the block until she saw her nephew, Angel, playing basketball with the neighborhood kids. She watched in silence as he stepped back and sunk the ball in the hoop. She jumped up and down in excitement.

"That's Ti-Ti's baby!"

His head snapped towards her before he took off running. "Ti-Ti!"

"Hi, my baby!" she squealed, as she bent over and picked him up. His little legs wrapped around his auntie's thick frame as they became reacquainted.

Esa and Sin were stagnant in their relationship. Because of that, Esa hardly saw her nephew outside of the monthly family dinners and FaceTime calls here and there.

Bliss was close with Sinaya up until about four years ago. It was like things shifted once Esa and Mario became serious.

They started to argue more and enter these periods where they wouldn't talk at all. It was all petty and childish to Bliss, and she couldn't understand why everything changed so suddenly.

Shaking the thoughts from her head, Bliss stared down at her handsome nephew. Taking in his deep dimples and bright brown eyes, she smiled and nuzzled him against her neck. "I missed you so much! Did you miss me?"

"Nah," he smirked.

"Oh, really?" she asked, giving him attitude. "That's how you feel?"

She began to kiss him all over his face causing him to laugh.

"Ti-Ti come on, yo," he said, trying to push her away. "Stop man," he said, while laughing.

"You know what you have to do," she replied, while never putting a stop to her annoying attack.

"Ok, ok Ti-Ti. I'm sorry." he said through giggles, "I missed you, too!" She finally stopped and gave him one last kiss on his forehead.

"Much better." She put him down and fixed his clothes.

Bliss played a game with the kids before going to stand by Junior's car, where she pulled her phone out and texted Junior, telling him to come outside.

\*\*\*\*\*

Bobbing along to Bob Marley, Esa passed the blunt back to Junior.

"Yo, ain't that Sin?" Junior asked, causing Bliss' head to follow where he was talking about. She was quiet as she observed her sister bend down into the passenger's side window of a black car.

"Fuck she going?" Bliss asked, as she watched her sister check her surroundings before hopping in the car. Bliss studied the car as it blended in with traffic.

If she wasn't mistaking, she would have thought that that was her ex's car. *Nah,* she thought to herself. What would they even have to talk about? Plus, her sister would tell her if she bumped into Mario.

Junior shrugged, blowing the smoke out of his mouth. "Not my bitch, not my business."

"Facts," Bliss agreed with a laugh.

Back inside of the cookout, Bliss had been avoiding Tyriq like the plague. She just wanted to relax today and not deal with any drama. She knew that Riq was going to go off on her for leaving the club without warning, and she didn't have the mental energy to deal with it.

Tyriq's eyes landed on Bliss before he signaled for her to come over to where he was.

"You better get over there before he makes a scene." Letty said, popping a chip into her mouth. The wonder twins, Esa and Letty, made up over a blunt and a couple of shots and were now snacking merrily together as if nothing ever happened.

"Don't be over there talking shit, Letty," Tyriq said.

"Boy, ain't nobody thinking about you." Letty rolled her eyes before walking to the door that led to the inside of the house.

"I better be all you thinking about. Where you going?"

"I'mma go to the store real quick. I gotta get some juice for the alcohol." Tyriq nodded, signifying that he understood before turning his attention back to Bliss.

Bliss sighed deeply before stopping in front of Riq. She knew he was about to go off about her neck.

She tried putting make-up on, but the bruise was so dark that she looked like she had two different skin tones on after all the cover-up she had to use. After trying and failing multiple times to cover it up, she just said fuck it. Everybody grilling her about it was gonna come either way.

She wore half of her curly hair out and let it hang so that she would be able to at least pose in a few pictures. The rest of her hair was up in a bun on top of her head. Her hair hanging just past her shoulders helped to cover up some of the bruises.

"Stop avoiding me Bliss, and bring ya ass over here."

"First things first, Bliss. You go with me anywhere, you leave with me. You stick with the herd, and that's final. If you tryna dip and do ya own thing, let somebody know, ya feel me?"

Bliss nodded solemnly. "Won't happen again brother. But just know that I am grown and can handle myself."

"I don't doubt that, but at the end of the day, I'm ya brother. It's my job to make sure you safe regardless of how old yo little ass is. And who you handling with yo fidget ass?" He cracked a smile before his eyes zeroed in on her neck.

"The fuck happened to your neck yo? I swear to God I'mma kill that nigga. Why the fuck you going around him anyway Bliss? Shit, I swear you bout to make me catch a body." He gulped from the red Solo cup that he was holding.

They sat down in a couple of beach chairs that was set up by the door to the house. "It wasn't Mario, Riq. I ain't been around him."

"Who was it then?"

"Yo Riq, I'm here." a familiar voice called from inside the house.

Bliss' head snapped up to the door as her skin began to tingle with electricity. Her heart rate sped up as she watched them walk out of the house.

"The fuck is you doing here?" Bliss stood up and yelled at the same time Junior did. He was standing next to Carlos at the grill when he looked over to check on Bliss.

Bliss snapped her head up towards Junior at the same time that he looked over to her. "You know him?" Junior asked her. She involuntarily took a step back and rubbed her bruised neck.

Realizing what she did, Bliss dropped her hand immediately before anyone could see. Looking at Junior, she knew that it was too late by the way he clenched his jaw.

"Yeah, I know her." Bent spoke. Flames were flying out of his eyes as he glared at Bliss.

Junior's eyebrows rose as he turned his fiery stare to Bent, "Oh, word?"

Bent looked over to Tyriq, "This the girl I was telling you about, Riq."

"Ohhhh...the crazy bitch from the oth-" he cut off mid-sentence and looked at Bentley. "Hol' up. So you the nigga that did this to her neck!?"

"Yeah, I did it. She was tryna steal from me. You know I don't play that shit." Bent answered Tyriq.

"Wasn't nobody stealing from yo ass Bent." Bliss spoke up as she looked at him for the first time. She noticed that he had a gash going across his forehead. It was a deep gash that was held together by stitches.

"Esa, come over here," Carlos said, peeping the tension that was flowing through the atmosphere. Bliss ignored him as she stared holes into Bentley's face.

"I see some shit don't change, huh, Bentley?" Junior said.

"Look, Junior," Bent began before Junior cut him off.

"Nah, you look at her fucking neck yo! You did this shit?" Junior yelled stepping towards Bentley.

"How you handle someone that steal from you June? She was tryna rob me." Bliss shook her head 'no' as Bentley kept accusing her. "Fuck you mean, no? I saw you with my wallet bitch!"

"Watch ya mouth!" Carlos yelled at the same time Junior pulled his gun out and aimed it at Bent.

"Give me one reason why I shouldn't murk ya lying ass right now." Junior said stepping forward.

Bliss' heart pounded in her chest as she walked towards Junior. "Junior, put the gun down."

"Don't touch me Bliss. I'm not playing."

"Benjamin, please. It's not worth it." she pleaded.

"He put his fucking hands on you, Esa!" Junior's hands tightened around the gun, "It's worth it."

"Is that the real reason why you wanna shoot me?" Bent asked Junior.

"Fuck you." Junior spat back.

"I can't take back what I did Junior." Bent replied calmly.

"Fuck outta here with all that bullshit you spitting!"

"I would if I could, June. you know I would. I lost a parent too."

"But not both!" Junior tensed and untensed his fist.

"Benjamin," Bliss said, walking closer to Junior. "Please baby, put the gun down." She stopped right in front of him. She could see the fire raging in his eyes as he kept the gun trained on Bentley.

She reached out and touched her hand to his face. She could feel his jaw clenching and unclenching. "Look at me." she said low enough for only him to hear. "June," she said softly, her tone pleading. "You promised."

"That was before I knew who it was." he spat out.

"Your word is your bond." Bliss said, while rubbing her thumb softly across his face. She released a breath that she didn't even know that she was holding, as he reluctantly lowered the gun.

Bliss reached up and kissed his cheek before kissing his lips softly. "Thank you, Junior." He pecked her lips once more before hastily walking out of the backyard.

# Chapter Eight

"Bent! Leave him alone." Bentley ignored Bliss, as he walked out of the front door after Junior.

*What the fuck just happened?* he thought, as he walked up the block in the direction that he thought he saw Junior walk in.

He made it to the corner when he felt a hand on his arm. Feeling the charged air and a jolt rock through his body, he already knew it was Esa. He hated that she had this effect on him, but he couldn't shake her.

"Junior is gone, a'ight? His car not even here, so you can quit searching for him." Bliss said to Bentley's back.

He sharply turned towards her, "So this was a setup the whole time, huh?"

"What are you talking about?" Bliss' eyebrows frowned up and furrowed in confusion.

"You 'bump' into me at the club, try to steal from me, get caught. Cut me with a fucking glass, and then, the very next day I'm brought to your house where you just kissed my brother after he pointed a gun at me."

"Brother? Fuck you mean?" her eyebrows dropped even lower as she ran the word repeatedly through her mind. *Brother? What the hell is this lunatic talking about?*

Bent smacked his teeth, "Don't act like you don't know."

She was so confused. She didn't know that Junior had any family outside of his Grandmother Lita. He never talked about anything; only thing he told her was that his parents died a while back.

"I seriously don't know what the hell you're talking about. And for the last fucking time, I wasn't stealing from your dumb ass."

"You had my wallet in ya hand."

"And you had a sonogram of my daughter. Where did you get it, huh? You cool with Mario or something? Did he put you up to this? Was fucking me a part of the plan, too, or was that just an added bonus for you?" Bliss fired off the questions as quickly as her mouth would allow.

Bentley looked at her like she was delusional, as he tried to understand what the hell she was talking about. He couldn't help but notice her hazel eyes blazing as she stared at him. "What are you talking about?"

"You threw your stupid wallet on the floor and all ya shit flew out. I picked it up for you when I saw this!" She smacked the sonogram against his chest. "This some kind of prank? Cause this shit not funny. How the fuck did you get this?"

He looked at the sonogram and was reminded of the girls he helped that day. His whole demeanor changed when he remembered feeling the girl's pregnant stomach move against his chest as he carried her to his truck. "I-I found it. You know who it belongs to?" He found the picture in his truck when he was cleaning the blood up. He didn't have the heart to throw it out, so he kept it.

She took a deep breath. "It's mine."

Bent's eyes snapped up to hers as his mind started to reel with so many thoughts, trying to make sense of what she was saying.

"Esa, you good?" Letty said, walking up to Bliss.

Bliss nodded, not taking her eyes off of Bentley.

"It's you." Letty said, stepping closer to get a good look at Bent. She thought he looked familiar, but the deep gash on his forehead threw her off. "I never got a chance to thank you."

"What you talking 'bout, Let?" Bliss asked. She had never been so confused in all of her life. She felt like she was in a twilight zone.

Bent showing up at her house was a big unexpected obstacle within itself. Everything that ensued after that just further added a flame to the gas leak.

"Wh-when I found you that day. I couldn't carry you down the stairs, so I went banging on the door next door. He helped and took us to the hospital."

Bentley felt the anger drain out of his body, as he thought about what Letty was saying. As things started to make sense, regret settled in the pit of his stomach. Flashes of him slamming Esa against the wall flashed through his mind.

"I gotta go." Bliss said, snatching the sonogram picture out of Bent's hand and turning to walk away. Bent grabbed her hand and pulled her back to him. She snatched her hand away roughly. "Don't touch me!"

Bent put his hands up as if to say that he surrendered. "My bad."

Bliss turned on her heel and walked away furiously. Instead of walking back towards her father's house, she went in the opposite direction and disappeared around the corner.

"Esa!" he called after her. When she didn't answer, he followed after her. "Esa! C'mere, let me talk to you for a minute." She kept walking like he hadn't even said anything. "Fuck!" he exclaimed running his hand through his dreads.

Turning around, he walked past a confused Letty and down the block towards the house. Hopping in his Range, he pulled out and mixed in with the city's traffic.

*****

Bentley was on his morning run in Brooklyn Bridge Park. He loved coming here early in the morning, because the park is empty, and he got to watch the sunrise. It was close to seven am and the sky was dark purple.

This was Bent's favorite thing to do with his dad and brother when their dad was alive. His dad was always up and out of the house before the crack of dawn at three am. The day after Bentley turned twelve, his father woke him up and told him to get dressed.

A couple months later, Junior joined them when he turned twelve. Even though Benjamin was married to Bentley's mom, Kat, Junior was a product of an infidelity.

According to what Bentley learned from Lita, Junior's mom, Alicia, came around proudly revealing her seven-month-pregnant belly at Kat's baby shower. They were due two months apart.

Benny took Bentley and Junior to an abandoned warehouse. The inside was converted to a gun range with all different types of weapons. He would give the boys daily lessons on how to use each one. He trained his sons to become beasts with the trigger. After the training was done for the day, Benny would stop and get Bent and Junior some breakfast and park close to the Brooklyn bridge to watch the sunrise before taking them to school.

This went on every morning until the day Benny was killed. They never missed a morning regardless of the circumstances or what they were going through. Even after the boys could shoot a target blindfolded from fifty feet away and not miss, they still met every morning.

If prison didn't teach him anything else, it was to appreciate the small things in life. He realized that he took a lot of things for granted before he got locked up.

For four years, he could not see the sunrise. That's why he got a place right next to the Brooklyn Bridge with floor to ceiling windows. With those windows, he could never miss another sun rise or set if he wanted to.

His mind drifted to his brother causing an ache to rift through his heart. Junior was his twin, and now, he didn't know if they would ever be close again. Shaking his head, he cleared his thoughts and focused on his run.

After completing his six-mile run, Bentley slowed down to a walk. He stopped at a food stand and purchased a water before beginning his walk home.

He saw a female by the park's lake taking pictures. His body charged with electricity, and he knew that it was Bliss. It had been a few weeks since the cookout, and this is the first time he's seeing her.

Walking over to her, he watched quietly as she snapped several pictures before checking them on her Nikon. He could tell she was in her element by the way she wasn't afraid to kneel on the ground or get close to what she was taking a picture of.

Looking at her after these few weeks they spent separated placed a small smile on his face. He knew what he had to do to make things right. Bentley wanted Bliss. He craved her laugh, her touch, her smell, and her taste. That one night he spent with her had his mind gone, and he couldn't get his mind off of her.

Bentley waltzed up to Bliss and wrapped his arms around her waist from behind. As her sweet scent filled his nostrils, Bentley relaxed. He felt her relax back against him before she snatched away.

"You got some nerve, Bentley," she said, without turning around to face him. She walked away and continued to snap her pictures.

"Lemme talk to you, Esa." She ignored him and stayed on the task at hand.

"Oh, so now you want to talk?" Bliss focused her camera on her target before taking a couple more shots.

"What's that's supposed to mean?" Bentley's eyebrows furrowed.

"The first time I tried to talk to you your hand was wrapped around my throat. You weren't tryna listen to a thief the second time either."

"I'm sorry, and I know that I fucked up-"

"Look, let's save the dramatics for another time. I have shit that I need to get done." Bliss checked the last few pictures on her camera. She was silently praying that he would just leave. She didn't feel like being bothered, and she definitely didn't have the energy to deal with Bentley.

Even after everything that went down, her knees weakened when she felt him close to her. She so badly wanted to turn around and throw herself into his arms, but he majorly violated, and she didn't know if there was any coming back from that.

Whatever little window of opportunity they had was closed and nailed shut.

"It's like that?" Bentley asked.

"That's how you made it. I don't even know why you came over here li-" She clamped her hand over her mouth as a wave a nausea hit her. She spotted a trash can nearby and ran towards it.

She made it just in time to bend over the trash bin before she began to violently vomit. Bentley rushed over there and grabbed her camera out of her hands before moving to the side.

After she was done, he handed her his bottle of water along with her camera.

"Thanks," she mumbled after taking a huge gulp.

He nodded, "You a'ight?"

She nodded as she finished off the bottle of water. Throwing the bottle in the trash, she said, "I gotta go, but I'm fine. Thanks for the water." She turned and walked off.

Despite feeling a little defeated, Bent walked away with a small smile on his face. She wasn't feeling the kid right now, but he could tell that she still felt something.

\*\*\*\*\*

"Uuuh," Bliss moaned before flushing the toilet.

She didn't want to plant the seed of her being pregnant in her head, but it was getting to the point where she couldn't deny it for much longer. She got up from her new home on the bathroom floor and brushed her teeth.

*What the fuck am I doing?*

She thought back to how this all started, the first of two times she and Junior had sex.

*Esa jumped up from the couch when the front door slammed closed. She had been waiting hours for Junior to finally come home after the monstrosity of a cook-out. She sealed off the blunt she had just finished*

116

*rolling before peaking her head around the corner to see what was taking
him so long to walk into the living room.*

*Esa watched as Junior stumbled into the living room before tripping
his way over onto the couch.*

*She could breathe now that he was home. She was worried about his
hot-headed ass being in the streets with an itchy trigger finger.*

*"You good?" she asked after watching him intently for a few minutes.*

*He popped up from the couch and crawled over to where Bliss was
standing a few feet away. He wrapped his arms around her thick waist
and hugged her close to him.*

*"I'm a'ight." Even on his knees, Junior threatened to be taller than
Bliss. He peeked up at her when she started to run her hands through his
hair. "You?"*

*She smiled faintly, "I'm a'ight." This was her fifth blunt since the
cookout, and it had her feeling really good, floating exactly how she
wanted to be. "You gonna tell me what's going on?" He shook his head
and squeezed her tighter to him. "You hungry?" she asked, still trying to
pick his brain.*

*"You know I am."*

*"I'll warm up ya plate," He gripped her waist tighter when she tried
to turn to walk away. She looked down at him puzzled. "What are you
doing?"*

*"Bout to eat." Junior lifted his t-shirt that she had on, and moved her
thong to the side.*

*"Oh, shit," Esa moaned softly when his warm mouth closed over her
sensitive flesh. She wanted to stop him so badly, but what he was doing to
her pussy was feeling too good.*

*"Junior, maybe we shouldn't."*

*Junior ignored her and went to work as he feasted on Esa's pussy. Each flick of his tongue melted another ounce of her resistance away. She was paralyzed as her first nut crept up her spine before washing over her.*

*"Fuck, Benny," she said, breathily, while pushing on his head to stop the sensual assault he was giving her body. He smacked her hand away as he continued to eat the soul out of her pussy.*

*"Mmm, shit" Esa moaned, when Junior began to fuck her with his tongue. The feeling of his stiff tongue moving in and out of her was driving her crazy. Her back arched as he worked her up until she was on the brink of exploding before he pulled away and stood up to his full height.*

*Junior laughed when she started whining. "I thought you wanted me to stop?" He pulled her into him and started caressing her ass.*

*"I never said stop."*

*"Word?"*

*She nodded her head, then he kissed her sloppily, his lips glistening with her essence. She traced her tongue across his lips, moaning at the taste of herself.*

*That shit drove him crazy with lust, "Keep it up; you gone get fucked."*

*Esa bit his lip, "Maybe, that's what I want." She wanted to feel good and not think about the day. She wanted to be some place the weed and alcohol couldn't take her. She wanted to feel free and let go, if only for a little while. She wanted to forget.*

He smirked down at her, "Suck this dick then, baby." He smacked her ass. She smiled before slowly sliding down his body until her knees hit the soft, plush carpet.

Freeing him from his jeans, Bliss' mouth watered at the sight of his thick, caramel-colored nine inches. She wasted no time licking the head of pre-cum up before taking all of his inches in her mouth.

"Fuck!" Junior yelled out when he touched the back of her throat. She pulled back and spit on it before deep throating it.

"Mhm, fuck it up, Ma." Junior moaned out.

Esa went harder hearing him lose his composure. "Mmmmm," she moaned when she looked up and saw that he was staring down at her, biting his bottom lip. Hallowing her cheeks in, she slowly pulled back until just the head remained in her mouth. She flicked her tongue in and out, around, and through his swollen mushroom while sucking hard.

She never broke eye contact with him.

"Fuck, get that shit, baby. Got damn." he praised her, as she made her way down before gagging. She stayed down with his head touching the back of her throat while caressing him with her tongue.

Before she knew what was happening, Bliss was on her back on the couch with Junior plunged deep inside of her.

"Fuck," they groaned collectively at the contact. Bliss wrapped her arms around his broad back. "Make me forget," she whispered in his ear.

He kissed her, "I got you." He told her to hold on, and that's exactly what she did while Junior took her on a euphoric roller coaster.

**Bang! Bang!**

Bliss snapped out of her flashback as her head whipped towards the bathroom door.

"Yo, you a'ight?" Junior's voice came floating through the closed wooden door. She shook her head clear from her thoughts and splashed some cold water over her face.

She pulled herself together before opening the door. "I'm fine; might have been something I ate earlier." She plopped down at the foot of his bed, face down.

Bliss felt and heard something land softly next to her head on the bed. Opening her eyes, she looked from the item up to Junior.

"Junior what-" Bliss started to say.

"When are you gonna stop lying to me, Esa?"

She looked down at the unopened pregnancy test. She was nowhere near ready to take this test. Instead of telling that to Junior, she said, "I really think it's something I a-"

"You been prancing around here claiming food poison and stomach bugs and shit when I know you carrying my seed. Stop fucking with me, Ma and take the test."

"I'm not taking this test." She got up and tried to leave the room.

"We not doing this storm out and leave shit. Take yo ass in there and use the bathroom before I make you do it myself."

Esa stared at him, and he stared right back, his expression not wavering.

She snatched the test out of his hands before miserably walking to the bathroom. She locked the door before falling against it and sliding to the floor. The reality of her possibly being pregnant hit her like a ton of bricks. She was still dealing with losing her baby. How was she supposed to be excited about being pregnant again?

Not only that, but if Bliss was pregnant, she was pregnant by Junior.

She knew that he was going to be an amazing father and that she wouldn't have to want for anything else, even though he's already taking care of her now. She should've been ecstatic that he even cared if she was pregnant or not. When she told Mario she was pregnant, he gave zero fucks; he even gave her money in case she wanted an abortion.

No matter how much she tried, she couldn't push the reoccurring thoughts of Bentley aside. When Junior touched her, she sometimes wished that it was Bentley's touch instead. She didn't want to, but she craved him.

"How long it take you to piss on a stick?"

Bliss jumped at the intrusion of Junior's voice in her thoughts. She completely zoned out on the floor in the bathroom.

"You need me to come in there?" Junior teased.

"Fuck outta here, June!"

"Well, hurry up and confirm what I already know."

She sighed deeply before heaving herself up off of the floor. Bliss forced herself to take the test before standing in the farthest corner away from it. Her breathing became shallow, as she stared at the small stick anticipating the timer to go off.

*Fuckity, fuck, fuck, fuck,* she thought as her phone announced that the three minutes were up. Her hands shook as she tried to pick it up.

The door creaked open seconds before Bliss felt arms wrap around her waist. "Yo you my baby moms, or not?" She looked at Junior through the mirror.

"How'd you even get in here?" she questioned with one brown raised.

"It's my house. Now answer my question." He kissed her on the neck before smiling wide at her. "Yes or no?"

His goofy grin was contagious as she told him, "I prefer the mother of your child."

"You dead ass?" She nodded as he kissed her forehead. "I told you."

She was quiet as her thoughts ran a mile a second. "I can't keep this baby, Junior," she whispered, before rushing past him and out of the door of the bathroom.

He snatched her back into him, "Fuck you mean? You better get over that shit real fast. You not killing my baby, Bliss." He left her in the hallway before going down the hall to his guest room, slamming the door shut.

Esa had him all the way fucked up. He was tight, listening to her stupid ass talk about killing his baby.

Junior was actually excited about her being pregnant. He loved Bliss. Yeah they weren't in a relationship, but she was family to him. He took care of her as if she was his lady. He loved being around her and spending time with her.

Junior could be himself and not have to have the weight of the world on his shoulders, and he loved being around Esa's energy. She was so pure and warm to him; she eased his mind with just the sound of her voice.

He was like a moth to her flame.

They became best friends in the months that they'd spent together, and Junior knew that Esa she was it for him. He just needed her to stop fighting him. He had liked her little ass back when she was with her donkey ass ex. He just wasn't sweating it like that, but he knew she would come to her senses eventually and leave Mario's ass.

Junior couldn't stay away from Esa if he tried. He didn't feel complete without his partner in crime. She was the cat to his dog. They didn't go anywhere without the other person.

He wanted Bliss.

Bliss was blowing him right now with her funky ass attitude though. He rolled up a few blunts before smoking two back to back. Esa had his nerves on edge right now, and he didn't want to argue with her simple ass.

Junior was in the middle of playing 2K when he heard his door creak open slowly. He didn't acknowledge her as he finished dunking with his customized avatar.

"You coming in or not, yo?" he said, impatiently towards the door. He kept the game going as she finally came in and sat her ass down. "You killing me Esa. I don't know what the fuck you need to do, but you need to get ya shit together. I do know that you better calm down, cause if my baby come out with his fingers where his toes at, I'm shooting you myself."

She giggled despite herself. "Shut up, June."

"I'm serious. You got me dumb tight with you talking about killing my baby. I don't preciate that shit. Dead ass."

Bliss bowed her head and let the tears fall. "Of course, I don't want to kill the baby, stupid. I'm just. I'm scared as hell right now."

He paused the game to look over at her. "I got you, Ma."

"I know you do."

"So, what you scared of?" He pushed her hair out of her face.

"I just am, a'ight? I couldn't even protect my first child; how I'mma protect this one?"

"Cause, I'm not a fuck nigga. I take care of mine. So put ya lip in, put ya feet up, and let daddy take care of the rest. Ya feel me?"

She rolled her eyes, "Yes, *Daddy,* I feel you."

He kissed her passionately. "I got you, Es."

"I know."

That's all he needed to hear for right now. Satisfied, he turned his attention back to the game.

She calmed down a little bit, but in the back of her mind, Bliss was worried about how Bent would react.

*Fuck him*, she thought to herself. He didn't care about her anyway. She made a mental note to block Bentley and remove him from her life.

For good.

Besides, she's having a baby with Junior. A man that actually cares about her. What more could she ask for? Right?

# Chapter Nine

*"The person you are trying to reach is not available."*

Bentley hit the end button in frustration as another one of his calls went straight to voicemail. It had been going on a few weeks since his run-in with Bliss at the park, and there was still no word from her.

He couldn't keep his mind off of her, and she had him in his feelings like a little bitch. Bent couldn't tell what spell she cast on him, but he was wishing that he handled shit differently.

After losing his father and going to prison, he didn't trust too many people. If any at all. His short fuse came into play whenever he thought that someone was trying to play him.

Bentley's heart dropped as he looked up at a picture of him, his father, and Junior that was sitting on his grandmother's mantle. They were all smiling at his granddad's 'Still Kicking' party. His grandad, Vernon, had a long battle with lung cancer, and it was finally in remission at the time, so they threw him a surprise party to celebrate.

Bentley looked at the next picture of Lita smiling while she was surrounded by her boys. She was never the same once Benny was killed. Bent going to prison that same day didn't help. On top of that almost a year later Vernon succumbed to the cancer. Bentley felt like shit that he wasn't there for Lita like he was supposed to be.

Now that he was out, he went to visit her every morning after his run. He would never let another day pass without him laying his eyes on his grandmother.

"Lo que está en su mente, Bebé Ben? Come talk to, Lita. What's on your mind?" Lita said from the kitchen.

Bent went into the kitchen and washed his hands before helping her to prepare breakfast. "What's the matter, mijo?"

Bent shook his head, "Nothing." She nodded her head in understanding. Lita knew that he would come and talk when he was ready.

After a little while in silence, Lita spoke up "Well, I've been thinking Baby Ben. I need to see my baby boys back together. It's been too long, and I hate that youse aren't talking."

"I tried-" Bent began but Lita cut him off.

"Yeah, I get that, but I'm not gonna be around forever Bentley Amir King. I would like to leave this earth knowing that my boys are on good terms, and at least talking. Youse is letting ya parents problems cause a rift between you, and that shit needs to stop."

"I don't know what you want me to do."

"Fix this shit, Bent. You all are all I have left, Bentley. Tell him the truth so that he can stop being bitter and begin to understand what really happened. How are youse supposed to heal if you don't talk about what happened. You all are brothers; you have a bond like nothing that this world has ever seen. Don't let the skeletons of your parents past continue to haunt you."

"I," Bent cut off to sigh deeply, "I don't know what you talking about old lady," he smiled. He didn't wanna talk about this right now and prayed that she left it alone.

"He deserves to know who really killed his mother. That boy is confused and angry, and you don't deserve all this hate. I get you wanna protect ya mother, Bent, but the truth is the truth."

"I hear you, Lita."

"Yeah, I know you do. I just hope that you're listening."

Bentley's phone began to vibrate in his pocket, causing him to quickly wipe his hands off and answer it. Anything to drop this conversation. He knew that even if he talked to his brother that they would always fight over Bliss.

"Yo," he barked into the phone.

"Meet me at the spot in twenty minutes, yo." Tyriq said on the other line.

"Bet."

Bent gathered his things before heading back to the small kitchen to kiss his grandmother on the cheek. "I'll be over here tomorrow."

"Remember what I said, Bent. Don't make me have to kick ya ass for you to listen to me."

He barked out a laugh, "I love you, too, Lita. I don't want those problems, Ma." He let the door slam behind him before locking the top lock and heading down the flight of stairs.

Bentley saw a man hanging on the rail in front of the building with a couple of other guys. The man that stood out had long hair and a Newport hanging out of his hand. He looked familiar, but Bent couldn't decipher where he knew him from.

The group became quiet as Bentley walked past them. Not paying them any attention, he continued his walk to his Range. He was a few feet away from the truck when one of the guys spoke up.

"Yo, you know Bliss?"

"Do I know you?" Bent asked, while turning around to face the group.

The man laughed before smirking. "Nah, but I know who you are."

"Is that right?" Bent's eyebrows rose.

"I'mma tell you this one time and one time only. I'm being nice cause I heard you just got out and shit, so you don't know the way it works around here. Bliss is my girl, so I advise that you stay away from her."

The thought of who it was went off in his head like a light bulb. Bent grinned, "You must be Mario."

"You know who the fuck I am, nigga." Mario barked back, as if Bentley was speaking to the president himself.

"Lucky guess, really. Let's just say your reputation precedes you. As far as her being ya girl?" Bentley smirked before chuckling, "If she was really your girl, she wouldn't have been screaming out my name as I fucked her brains out from the back while smacking that fat ass." he barked out a laugh, "Go on bout ya business playboy."

"I'mma see you around." Mario said staring daggers into Bentley.

"You know exactly where to find me." He got into his truck and pulled off.

\*\*\*\*\*

"Yo ass done went to prison and got some nigga superpowers or some shit." Tyriq said squatting down, gulping his Gatorade.

Bent and Tyriq were just finishing the last of several one on one games. They were at the basketball court in Tyriq's neighborhood. Bent won three out of the five games that were played, not including the two they won when they were playing in teams against other dudes from the park.

"Shut yo crybaby ass up. You just mad cause you got whooped, nigga," Bent said wiping his forehead with his shirt. He took it off and wrapped it around his head like a bandana.

"You only won because I let you."

Bent barked out a laugh. "What game was you playing? I dusted that ass, boi."

"Yeah, whatever my G." He gulped his Gatorade. "So any progress in the situation with Esa?"

"Hell no," He plopped down on the bench and started twirling the basketball in his hand. "I saw her a little while back, but she wasn't feeling the kid."

Tyriq nodded to let him know that he was following along. "I get why, though. The shit that popped off between you was fucked up my nigga." Tyriq spoke up. Esa was like a little sister to him. They had grown really close in the past two years that he and Letty had been dating off and on.

"I regret the way I handled that shit, but what can I do about it now, ya feel me?"

"Look, you my boy so I'mma keep it a hunnid with you. Shit run deep with her, so you gotta tread carefully. I had to fuck her nigga up a few times for putting his hands on her, ya feel me?"

Bent was quiet as he listened to what Tyriq had to say. He thought back to what Letty said that day. Could it really be possible that Bliss was the girl that he was looking for the whole time?

"I ain't mad though. People fuck up. Esa just went through a lot so she guarded. Give her time to come around." Tyriq continued.

"Man, that shit over with." Bent brushed it off. "It's whatever." Bent knew deep down that his words didn't ring true to even his own ears. Tyriq knew as well, but he wasn't gonna call his homie out on it… not yet, anyway.

"You wanna get that ass whooped again or you calling it a night?" Bent stood up and began dribbling the ball.

"Fuck what you heard; I'm the king of these streets, nigga. I'll break ya ankles all up and down this mufucka."

"Put ya skills where ya mouth is, nigga. D-up."

Bent and Riq were deep in the game when they heard yelling. They ignored it, chucking it up to be the regular noises of the park and kept playing until the yelling grew louder.

It sounded like a couple of girls arguing and yelling. Tyriq stopped playing to see where the arguing was coming from; he was on high alert.

"You good, Riq?" Bent asked, jogging over to Riq.

"That sound like my girl." He looked around until he saw something and headed in that direction. He ran over to the other side of the courts with Bent following close behind. They got there just in time to see all hell break lose.

Bliss and Letty were dragging two girls on the sidelines.

Bliss knocked the girl she was fighting with down before hopping on top and wailing on her face.

Letty had one girl by the hair while punching her in the face.

They peeped two dudes hanging on the sidelines, inching closer to the girls. One dude went in and grabbed Bliss off the top of the girl before flinging her to the side. Bentley saw red as he ran towards the dude and made his fist connect to the man's face.

He put dude to sleep with two punches. When he looked up, he saw just as Tyriq gave a mean right hook to a guy's chin. Seeing that Riq was cool, he looked over to find Bliss and saw her back on top of the girl that she was beating up before.

Bliss was deathly silent as she rained blows on the girl's face. She began to slam the girls head onto the concrete floor. Adrenaline pumped through her veins like lava as she finally scratched that annoying little itch. Bent went over there and grabbed Bliss up while pinning her arms to her side.

"Talk that shit, now, bitch! Fuck with me if you want to. You already got that ass beat once before hoe. Learn how to stay the fuck down." she yelled, as Bent attempted to escort her away from the chaotic scene.

"Come on, Esa. Let's go."

"Let me go, Bent. I ain't going nowhere with you, and I'm definitely not done with that bitch!"

"If you want ya little slut to keep her life, I suggest you keep her locked up." Rasheeda, the girl that Bliss was fighting, spoke up and said as Bentley carried Bliss in the opposite direction.

"Fuck all that talking shit; let me go!" Bliss struggled against his grasp until she finally broke free.

Her mind went blank as her fist connected to Rasheeda's skull. Each hit was harder than the last. She was locked in on her target and wasn't going to stop until her enemy was eliminated.

Rasheeda fell down to the ground under the force of Bliss' blows. Bliss stuck to her like glue, never stopping her parade of punches.

Next thing she realized, she was flying in the air. She didn't know who had her so she kept swinging.

"It's me, Esa. Stop swinging." Bentley's voice finally broke through, causing Bliss to wake up from her blackout.

She stopped swinging and struggling against him as she looked around. She saw the girl she was fighting was struggling to stand up, but she fell down, then still continued to try to get back up to her feet.

Bliss smirked at the sight as Bentley picked her up. She wanted to yell, "Stay down, bitch!" But she decided that she let her hands do enough talking for her today.

"Let me get you out of here before I gotta fuck somebody baby mama up for trying to jump you." He carried her away from the chaos before putting her down. "I'll take you wherever you wanna go."

Bliss looked up and saw that Riq was dragging Letty off the court kicking and screaming about how she had to finish the job. Knowing how Riq and Letty were, she knew they would end up fucking against somebody's car.

She knew her options were limited, but being around Bentley was something that she didn't want to do.

"I'll get home." Bliss said, before turning and walking away. She made it to the sidewalk before he caught up to her.

"Bliss!" he yelled out.

His deep baritone froze her steps and chilled her down to her bones. She stopped walking but did not turn around to face him. He strode over to her, stopping just a few feet away. "I'm just tryna talk to you."

"I don't need, nor do I want to talk with you, so leave me alone Bentley." She began her walk again before he stopped her by grabbing her arm gently.

That unwavering spark sizzled up her arm, causing her heart to skip a beat.

"I can't stop thinking about you, Bliss. I don't even have to see you to know when you're near me." He turned her around to face him, then lifted her face with his fingers to make her look him in the eyes. "I know you feel this shit, Ma."

"It doesn't matter what or how I feel. I don't want anything to do with you!!" She snatched away from him.

He only pulled her closer to him before kissing her.

Bliss stood rigidly as she tried to fight against the sensations that surged through her body. He placed one hand in her hair and gently scratched against her scalp.

Moaning, Bliss gave in and kissed him back. This was all that she could think about the past few weeks. As much as she hated to admit it, she couldn't keep the time that she spent with Bent out of her mind.

Kissing her one final time, Bent broke the kiss. "I want you, Bliss. I'm not gone stop till I have you."

She looked him in the eyes and saw that he was serious. She wanted him, too, but they were already off to a rough start. She couldn't leave one bad thing just to hop back into another.

She couldn't do Junior like that either.

She was about to reply when gunshots rang out nearby. Bentley pulled his gun out and pushed Bliss behind him. He pulled his keys out and gave them to her.

"Go and get in the truck. It's a few cars down. I'll be back. Don't move till I get here."

"Fuck that, I'm going with you."

"Bliss, just get in the damn truck! I don't have time to be out here arguing with you."

"I said no."

Seeing the determination on her face, Bentley relented, "Man, a'ight, come on." He was pissed off that she would pick right now to argue. He couldn't afford to be worried about her, too.

His mind was on getting to them niggas that was shooting. His gut was telling him that those bullets were intended for him and his crew.

They ran up the block through the crowd of screaming people. They knew that they had made it to their destination when they saw Tyriq and Letty firing off rounds at a car that floored it up the street and away from the flying bullets.

"You straight?" Bent asked once the car was out of sight.

"Yeah, we good. Yall good?" Tyriq asked.

"We straight, yo." Bent answered, before turning on Bliss and grabbing her face in between his fingers. He held on tight enough to where he had control, and she couldn't break free.

"If you ever pull some shit like that again I will smack the shit out of you. Do you understand me?"

Bliss jumped at the ferocity in his voice. "You talking to me?" she asked, before she could think about it.

"Who the fuck else am I talking to, Bliss? You smart, baby girl. Come on, now." The little bit of patience that he had left was quickly disappearing. It was as if she was tap dancing on his nerves with stilettos on. He was trying not to spazz at her already and dealing with her smart ass mouth was something he wasn't about to do.

"If some shit ever pop off, I need you to do what the fuck I tell you to do. I'm telling you to do it for it a reason. What it look like with you standing there arguing with me and gunshots is ringing off in the background? What if one of them bullets came and hit you or me while we standing there bickering? That shit is childish. Don't do it again."

She was quiet. Her wide eyes staring at his fiery gaze.

She dropped her stare down to his lips. She couldn't help but clench her pussy muscles when his tongue peeked out and wet them. Him taking control had her fighting against every urge in her body that wanted to fuck him senseless right here and now.

"Are we clear?" his deep baritone rang through her naughty thoughts.

She nodded her head before speaking softly, "Yes."

"Good." He dropped his hand from her face. "Let me rap with you real quick, Riq." He said turning away from Bliss to face Tyriq.

Tyriq nodded his understanding before turning towards Letty, "Go get in the car, Letty." She looked at him like he had lost his mind. "Just go, Letisha. I'm not in the mood to be arguing with yo ass. I'll be there in a second." He kissed her forehead before she dejectedly made her way to Riq's truck.

"I'mma go and check on her real fast." Bliss spoke up.

"Bliss," Bent called after her. She stopped and looked at him, waiting for him to continue. "We leaving in a minute so don't go too far." She started to say something back to him, but the look on his face silenced all of her arguments. She merely nodded before jogging to catch up with Letty.

Riq smirked at Bent as they watched Bliss walk away. He started laughing when Bentley smacked his teeth.

"I don't even wanna hear it, yo." Bent tried to control the grin that slowly spread across his face and failed miserably. He was still tight with her short ass, but she was so damn beautiful. Especially, with her lips poked out because her feelings were hurt.

He didn't know whether he wanted to laugh at her, curse at her, or break her off with some of that good pipe.

"Anyway, so what's up?" Bent asked getting back to business.

"Them the same pussy ass niggas that we dusted up on the court when B and Letty was knocking them bitches out." Tyriq fumed.

"Word?" Bentley's eyebrows rose up, "They was big mad huh?"

"Man, hell yeah. It's a'ight, though I know where they at."

"Word?"

"Facts. They run with ole dude that questioned you about Bliss and shit, her ex or whatever. This nigga is a straight pussy. He not gone fight you head on. He a snake. What he gone do is get you where you least expect it. but I already got my nigga on it."

Bentley nodded his head, soaking in the new information. "Let me know something."

"Bet, I got you."

"One," They dapped each other up before making their way to where the girls were before each couple went their own way.

Bliss was quiet as she rode in Bent's Range. She had so much on her mind that she felt like she was drowning. She could feel Bent's stare burn her face every once in a while, but other than that, he kept quiet, which she was thankful for.

She could feel her resolve breaking, and that was a no Bueno. As soon as they got to their destination, she planned on dipping. She didn't need to be around him any longer.

She didn't know how much longer she could fight against him. Fight against the feelings that evoked with every thought of him. He evaded her thoughts and her senses … he consumed her whole being.

She was slowly losing this battle.

Esa was damaged, and it was best if she just stayed away. Plus, it was always chaos whenever they were in the same space. Who wanted to live like that?

With her being pregnant now, she doubted he wanted anything to do with her anyway.

She closed her eyes and took a deep breath, then she felt his hand cover hers gently, before he squeezed it and linked their fingers together. She felt a sense of calm overcome her as her body relaxed back against the seat.

"Just remember that I get what I want, Bliss." She looked over at him as he kissed her hand. "And I want you."

Deep down. She knew she wanted him too.

## Chapter Ten

"It seems as if a congratulations are in order." Bliss' OB doctor said coming into the room. "Congrats, Mom and Dad." Dr. Brown smiled at them.

Bliss nervously looked over at Junior. He smiled before kissing her forehead. "We already knew that though. The way I busted that thing wide open, I won't be surprised if there's two in there."

Bliss' face turned red before the giggles started. "Junior!"

"Man, you know it's true."

Dr. Brown laughed, "Do you have any questions so far? Bliss, you're kind of quiet today." Dr. Brown has been her OB/GYN since she turned sixteen, so he knew her very well.

"Is there any chances of my baby not making it?" She asked the question that had been plaguing her mind day and night. She couldn't bring herself to be happy over this pregnancy if she was going to lose this baby too.

She knew she was over exaggerating, but this fear was paralyzing. Bliss knew that the reason why she lost Cielo was because of what Mario did to her; she just couldn't bring herself to let the fearful thoughts go.

"Are you asking in reference to your previous pregnancy?" Bliss nodded her head. "I believe you will be fine. There was a cause for the placental abruption. Meaning that it did not happen naturally. You will be closely monitored though. So hopefully that will ease some of the hesitation you might feel towards being pregnant."

Bliss exhaled slowly before her eyes welled up with tears.

Junior placed his arm around Bliss' shoulder. "Aye, Doc, can you give us a minute?"

"Sure thing. I'll be back in a few."

"'Preciate it."

Once the doctor was gone, Junior kissed Bliss on her forehead. "As long as my body is on this earth, Ima make sure that our baby survives. There's no need to worry baby girl. I got you."

Bliss allowed the tears to fall as she tried to get her anxiety to subside.

Junior didn't say anything as he wiped her tears. This was nothing new to them. Ever since he witnessed her having a panic attack, this had become their routine. He would just talk to her until she was calm enough to respond back. It happened more frequently than not, especially if she had the same reoccurring nightmare about her baby girl.

Taking a few deep breaths, Bliss calmed down enough to stop the tears. "Thank you, Benny."

He kissed her before wrapping his arms around hers in an embrace. He felt her relax against him.

Hearing a knock on the door, Junior pulled away and walked to the opposite side of the examination table, still remaining close to Bliss.

Dr. Brown walked in with some papers and small packages. "Here's some information about the first trimester and what to expect. I also have some samples of prenatal vitamins for you."

Bliss thanked the doctor and put everything into her purse before settling back in the bed.

"Would you all like to hear your baby's heartbeat?"

Bliss' eyes expressed her confusion as she spoke, "I thought you could only hear it when you're at least six weeks a long?"

"Honey, you're nine weeks."

Bliss' eyes grew wide as she started to mentally do some calculations. "Really? nine weeks?"

"Yes, lay back for me."

Bliss followed instructions as the doctor prepared the exam.

*Nine weeks?* she thought to herself. She was further along in her pregnancy than she originally thought. Her all day sickness only started a few weeks ago, so she thought that she was around four weeks. That lined up with the second and last time that she and Junior had sex.

She knew for sure that Junior was the father.

Now … she's not so sure anymore.

Bliss' eyes welled up with tears when the whooshing sound of her baby's heartbeat filled the room. She looked up at Junior whom was smiling. "So that's my baby's heartbeat? That shit is mesmerizing."

"Strong and healthy, isn't it?"

"Hell, yeah," he grinned. "That shit is crazy yo."

Hearing the heartbeat made it real for Bliss. She released a breath and relaxed further. Junior kissed her on her forehead, before pulling out his phone and recording a quick video.

*****

Bliss walked into the room after her shower. She had one of Junior's high school hoodies on and some spandex shorts. She put her hair up into a bun before joining Junior on the bed.

He wrapped his arm around her shoulder and brought her closer as he turned the TV to ESPN.

"June, there's something I have to talk to you about."

"It can't wait till after Sports Center?"

She smacked him upside his head. "You serious, right now?" she said sitting up.

Junior laughed before turning the TV volume lower, so that she wouldn't have to scream.

"A'ight, a'ight, speak ya mind shorty."

"I'm-" She paused to take a deep breath. "I'm not one hundred percent sure that the baby is yours."

His head snapped towards her; his eyes connecting instantly with hers. The look he gave her crushed her into a million pieces. If looks could kill, she would be dust particles. "The fuck you talking about?"

"I'm nine weeks. That means that I would have gotten pregnant around my birthday weekend."

146

"The fuck that gotta do with anything Bliss? Quit stalling and spit that shit out, yo." He grew irritated.

"I slept with Bent the night of my birthday."

"You what?" He stuck his head in her direction, as if to say he couldn't hear her.

"I slept with Bentley on my birthday." she said more loudly, even though she knew that he heard her the first time.

Junior slid to the end of the bed with his back facing Bliss. "I never pegged you for a hoe and a liar."

"Excuse me?" Her head jerked back as she looked at him in bewilderment.

"You heard me."

"I get that you're upset right now, but that's no reason for you to call me out of my name, Junior."

"Fuck outta here, Bliss. You just told me that my seed that you're carrying may not be mine, and it might be my brother's. That's some hoe shit! No matter how you try to flip, switch, or turn that shit." Junior's mind was racing a mile a minute. His heart hurt, and he didn't know how to handle that so he became angry.

"Fuck you, Junior!" she yelled as she slid off of the bed, not being able to sit down any longer. Her heart was beating rapidly as her adrenaline began to pump through her body.

"Oh, so it's fuck me?" he yelled back at her. He hopped off of the bed and turned to face her. "Fuck you!"

He couldn't believe what the fuck was happening. His blood was burning hot as his fuse became shorter.

"At least I'm keeping it real with you. I'm not leading you on."

"You could've kept that shit to ya self, Ma!" His grip on his sanity was loosening fast.

"And what would happen seven months from now if the baby happens to look more like him than you? You would really be calling me a liar for keeping it from you!"

"Fuck man!" Junior yelled before punching the wall. He could feel himself begin to explode. He knew that, if he didn't get out of there soon, he would hurt her.

Bliss jumped at hearing the impact his fist made into the drywall. She took an instinctive step back, even though he was across the room.

"I'm not tryna hurt you, Junior. I'm trying to keep it a hundred with you. I ain't never lied to you, before, and I'm not about to start now."

Junior barked out a laugh, "Yeah, right. You lying is what got us here." He was pacing back and forth, trying to expend some of the aggression that he was feeling.

Bliss blew out an irritated breath, "What did I lie to you about?"

He stopped pacing to look at her. "You dead ass? How about the fact that you fucked the nigga!"

"You never asked, I never told. I figured if you wanted to know, you would ask."

"You not telling me is the same fucking thing as lying, Bliss. Do you not hear ya self?" He pinched the bridge of his nose before turning swiftly and going into the closet.

"Do you tell me when you sleep with other bitches?" Bliss yelled out after him. She waited for a response and never got one. "Exactly my point, Junior!"

He appeared in the doorway of the closet. "This is about a baby, Bliss, not who I'm fucking. You don't think I should have known that there was a possibility that your kid ain't mine before I was running around looking like a fucking idiot? Playing proud papa and shit going to the appointments. The fuck I look like?"

"Why the fuck do you think I'm telling you now, Junior? Do you really think I would have come to you if I wasn't sure? As soon as I put the shit together, I told you! That should say something to you."

"A'ight," He waved his hand dismissively before walking back into the closet.

Bliss followed after him.

"I can't get dressed alone?" he said without turning to face her.

Her face fell, "Where are you going?"

He turned to look at her, "Fuck you care for? Just get out of my face right now, Bliss."

"I'm just tryna-" Bliss began.

"Look," he cut her off. "I just need some space right now, yo."

"So what you saying? You want me to leave?"

"Take it how you want to. Do you. You not my bitch; it's not my business." He shrugged, never stopping his task at hand.

Bliss nodded her head before retreating from the walk-in closet. She was boiling mad as she put on her Timbs, grabbed her shoulder bag, and left Junior's apartment with the door slamming behind her.

So many thoughts were running through her mind as she made her way to Letty's. It was a thirty-minute walk to Letty's house, and Bliss was grateful for it. She could use the time to herself and blow off some of this energy.

She wanted to believe that this was just a rough patch between her and Junior, but she wasn't sure if their friendship could survive after this. Tears formed in her eyes as her heart panged with sadness. *What The fuck?! Fuck, fuck, fuck!* She felt like she was about to lose it.

Bliss didn't know how Junior was going to react; she knew it wasn't going to be good, but she never expected that.

Esa's emotions were all over the place. She didn't know whether to cry, scream, fight, or curl up in a bed and never come out. She was lost.

What she really wanted was a blunt, a strong drink, and some restful sleep without nightmares.

She wanted to be happy that she was pregnant. She wanted to *want* her baby. She wanted to hug her baby girl Cielo. She wanted to smile and be happy and not pretend.

She didn't have the energy to pretend like everything was good anymore.

Her thoughts roamed to Bentley and a small smile graced her face before falling slightly.

She didn't know how he was going to react to her news, but she had to tell him. She may be in a messed up situation right now, but she wasn't a trifling female. Until she was far a long enough in her pregnancy to get a DNA test, they'd both just have to suck up any ill feelings and be involved.

Esa rolled her eyes at her own naïve and far-fetched idea. She couldn't even get Junior to sit down and have dinner with Bentley for Lita. There was no way he was going to be a willing participant in her pregnancy trio. Especially not after tonight.

She sighed deeply and decided to call Bent on her walk to Letty's to see if they could meet up soon. She hadn't spoken to him since the basketball court shenanigans a few weeks ago.

She was met with his voicemail, so instead of leaving a message she hung up and sent him a text.

Getting to Letty's Condo, Bliss kicked off her shoes by the front door and went straight to her room. She dove under the blankets and watched a few episodes of *The Walking Dead* on Netflix before falling into a restless sleep.

# Chapter Eleven

After waking up to find Letty cuddled up behind her, Bliss cooked breakfast for the both of them before finally calling Bentley again. She saw that he read her message but didn't send a response.

Getting his voicemail, again, she grew irritated and decided to go to his house.

"Need me to go in with you?" Letty poked her head into Bliss' room while she was getting dressed.

"Nah, I should be good."

"A'ight, you know I don't play about my girl. Especially, since you're carrying my child." Letty said, rubbing Bliss' stomach.

"Calm down, Baby Daddy." Bliss giggled, "I don't think he's going to try anything since he got those stitches."

Letty fell out laughing, "You cracked that nigga skull down to the white meat. My girl was playing no games. I bet that ass will think twice next time."

"I bet you he will." Bliss smirked.

\*\*\*\*\*

**Bang! Bang! Bang! Bang!**

Bliss banged on Bentley's door once more. She had been standing out here knocking politely for the past five minutes, but that didn't get her anywhere so she graduated to banging.

She picked her fist up to bang again when the door swung open. She was met with a female, and the girl had her nose turned up like she smelled something foul. Bliss looked the girl up and down taking in her wrinkled appearance. She could give credit where it was due and say that the girl was pretty, despite the ugly look on her face.

"Can I help you?"

Bliss brushed past the girl and made her way into the house. "You can't, but he can, so I'm not here for you. Thanks for offering, though." Bliss walked up the hallway towards Bent's room.

"You can't just barge in like that!" the girl screamed after her.

Bliss ignored the girl and went into his room. She went right over to him and mushed his face before stepping back. "Get up!"

He looked so cute, like he was sleeping peacefully. She hated to disturb him, but she was on a mission.

"What the fuck!" Bent woke up swinging as he sat up swiftly. He thought he was bugging when his eyes landed on Bliss. "Esa?"

He wiped the sleep from his eyes. "Fuck are you doing here? What time is it?" he croaked out.

"We need to talk." She turned on her heel and walked out of his room.

Bent sat on the edge of his bed trying to get his bearings. *What the fuck yo?* he thought to himself.

Bent was in the bathroom taking care of his hygiene when he heard arguing. "What the fuck man?" he sighed deeply before quickly finishing his task of brushing his teeth. He slipped on some shorts before going up the hallway.

"Bitch, you can't kick me out, so until he come and ask me to leave, I'm not going nowhere." the girl said to Bliss as she played on her phone.

"Oh, really?" Bliss' eyebrows rose up in astonishment.

"What's going on?" Bentley asked, announcing his presence. It didn't escape his attention how Bliss' eyes roamed over his bare tattooed chest.

"So glad that you could join us." Bliss spoke up. "I was just walking your company to the door."

Bent barked out a laugh, "Word?" He stared down at Bliss. She stared up at him not missing a beat. Bent could tell that she was serious, but he wanted to see how far he could push her. "I can speak for myself, Es. I'll ask her to leave when I'm ready. After all, I did ask her to stay."

He watched as her poker face fell a little before her lips evened out into in a thin line. *God damn, her little short ass is fucking beautiful,* he thought to himself as he drunk in her whole body slowly.

"Look, I don't have time for games. Get rid of the bitch or I will."

"Who you calling a bitch?" The girl started to walk towards Bliss. "I will fuck,"

Bliss smacked the girl before she could finish her sentence. She lunged forward to finish the job, but Bent grabbed her before she could sink her nails into the girl.

"You doing too much talking for me, bitch." Bliss said smirking.

"Man, come on with that bullshit." Bent complained, as he carried Bliss down the hallway. The other girl ran after them and started swinging around Bentley. Bliss saw this and tried to fight back, but Bentley pushed her away at an arm's length.

He had the other girl pushed back as well. "Man, chill the fuck out." He pushed Bliss into his room and slammed the door before pushing the girl up the hall towards the door.

"Look, let me handle this. You gotta go." He handed her a few blue benjis. "Take a cab, and by ya self something nice. I'll hit you up later."

"You need to train your pets." she said, snatching the money from him.

"Shut ya mouth before I sic her on you." he told her, causing her to roll her eyes. "Hurry up and get out." He slammed and locked the door behind her before stalking down the hallway.

Bentley was irritated, but the whole situation was amusing to him. If he didn't know before, he knew now that she wanted him.

"You can't just barge in here slapping bitches like that, Esa."

"I asked her to leave nicely. The bitch jumped stupid." she said, nonchalantly.

"This is not your house. You can't dictate what happens over here."

"Look, I asked you to meet up with me so we can talk like adults, but you wanted to ignore me."

"I was obviously busy."

"And this is obviously important, Bentley." She placed her hand on her hip.

"If you wanted to spend time with the kid all you had to do was ask." he smirked.

"I'm pregnant." Bliss blurted out before she could lose her nerve. She watched his smirk slowly fade off of his face. "There's a possibility that you are the father."

"Possibility? So you don't know?"

Bliss wanted to go and hide from embarrassment, but instead, she held her head up high. "It's between you and Junior."

Bentley's heart dropped hearing the news. He figured he would be hearing from her soon about this ever since he witnessed her throwing up at the park. He didn't imagine that there would only be a possibility. Especially not between him and his brother.

"Fuck," he said wiping his hand over his forehead before plopping down on the couch at the foot of his bed. "You told Junior?"

"Of course," She fought the urge to roll her eyes

"How did that go?"

"The pregnancy part went well. The possibility part, not so well."

"I hope you ain't come over here to tell me to leave you alone. Cause I can tell you now that shit not bout to work."

"Why would I do that?" She was genuinely surprised by his statement.

"Cause you with Junior." He hopped up and moved towards her.

"I'm not with anybody." Her voice was quiet as the energy in the room shifted.

The sexually charged tension was so thick that Bent couldn't think straight. His body yearned to be near hers. He needed to feel her soft hips in his hands. He yearned to bite his spot on her neck. He had to feel her lips against his. He urged to be deep inside of her. Everything about her was singing to him, summoning him to be near her.

"But you live with him?" he asked, while continuing his stride towards her.

"What you stalking me or something?" She backed up slowly.

"I know everything where you're concerned."

Her eyebrows rose, "Oh, really?"

"I already told you once, I get what I want Esa. I made it clear that I want you." Bliss swallowed hard as Bentley closed the distance and backed her smooth against the wall.

His dreads hung loosely past his shoulders tempting her to run her hands through them. Bliss had to restrain herself from reaching out and touching them.

*Good Lord, why does he have to be so close? Take the wheel, Jesus,* she thought to herself, as his scent surrounded her and made love to her nostrils. His spicy scent made her mouth water with want for him.

"I know you want me, Esa. Otherwise, you wouldn't have smacked that girl."

He started laughing when she smirked. "You don't even know her name."

"Does it matter? The only name I need to know is yours." He inched his head down to hers. Looking her in the eyes, he said, "I'm sorry for what I did to you, Bliss." His hands found their way around her waist. "Let me prove it to you." He kissed her once. "I'mma make sure you won't regret it." He kissed her once more.

"I'mma hold you to your word." she said looking him dead in the eyes.

"Don't even worry 'bout all that. I got you." he said, smiling, before lowering his lips to hers once more.

They moaned in unison at the satisfaction of giving into the connection that they were craving. She never wanted to deny him again; it took too much out of her. To keep fighting against him was like trying to fight against your body's natural ability to breathe by itself.

Esa could never get used to the feeling that he caused to travel through her body. He gripped her ass tightly and lifted her up until her legs wrapped around him, and he felt like he couldn't get enough.

Bent reluctantly pulled away when he thought he heard knocking. "Yo, you hear that?" They listened, and sure enough, the persistent knocking continued. "Fuck, man. Who is it now?"

He kissed Bliss passionately before letting her slide down his body. "Don't move. I'm coming back."

She giggled, "Where am I going?" Bent smirked before leaving the room.

"Who the fuck is it?" he asked, peeping through the peephole. When he didn't see anything, he pulled out the gun he had stashed away in the kitchen. The banging started up again, so Bent aimed his gun and swung the door open.

He was met with the barrel of a gun, and he burst out with laughter. "We gotta stop meeting like this." He stepped to the side and allowed Letty into the house.

"Where she at? Bliss?!" Letty yelled.

"Let?" Bliss could be heard coming up the hallway.

"Bliss!"

"What are you doing here?" Bliss asked going over to her best friend.

"You wasn't answering your phone, yo. You good?" She looked Bliss over to make sure she didn't see anything wrong with her or out of place. Once she saw that everything was ok she tucked her gun away.

"I'm good." Bliss genuinely smiled at her.

"You ain't have to cut nobody, I see."

Bentley chuckled before grabbing a laughing Bliss in a headlock, with his arm around her shoulder.

"Nah, but I did have to smack a bitch."

"About that, I'mma need yo pregnant ass to stop fighting. That's the second one that I've seen in the last few weeks." Bent spoke up. He placed his arms around her waist and gently dropped his hands to her stomach.

The feeling that she felt standing there in that man's arm caused her heart to surge with an overwhelming sense of love. It was like a lock clicking into place for Bliss. She knew that that was where she belonged.

Bentley bit his spot on Bliss' neck causing her body to shudder involuntarily. "Don't make me have to fuck you up if my baby come out retarded cause you can't control ya anger." He bit his favorite spot again, before licking over it to soothe the sting. Bliss moaned out as her need for him increased.

"That's my cue to go. I'll be downstairs in the car," Letty said, placing her index finger straight up, as if she was excusing herself in church, before walking out of the door.

"Keep your toys in they place, and you won't have any problems from me." Bliss turned around in his arms, before placing hers around his neck.

Bent barked out a laugh. "Be dressed and ready by eight tonight, and I'll donate my toys to Goodwill."

"They better be donated and forgotten way before then." She said, as she looked him square in the eyes. Her hazel eyes showed the fire that her words carried.

Bent smiled; he loved her feistiness.

She wasn't scared to say how she felt and that was a major turn-on. "What I tell you earlier? I got you. I meant that, a'ight?"

Bliss smiled shyly. "Ok." Just like that, her fire was tamed for now.

He grinned back at her, "Come here." He guided her head closer to his where he kissed her. "I'm serious, Bliss. Trust me." He gave her a couple stacks before smacking her ass. "I'll see you later."

"Bentley!" she gasped before giggling.

"You like that shit."

"Maybe." she said, smirking as she walked out of the door.

## Chapter Twelve

"Where to?" Letty asked once they were seated in her truck.

"Seems like I have a date later so Kings Plaza?" Bliss asked, trying to contain her smile.

"Yes, bitch! I see you, Mama." Letty said, showing her excitement about Bliss going on a date. "You told him everything?"

"Yeah. He handled it way better than I could have imagined."

"I like him for you, B. I'm happy that you're giving him a shot."

"It's just a date, Letty. I'm not marrying the kid."

"Yet." Letty said under her breath.

"Oh, whatever!" Bliss laughed.

"I'm Team Bentley. Don't get me wrong I love Junior. I think youse are good together, but he doesn't give you that spark. Youse will be awesome parents, but anything outside of friends? I don't see it." Letty told her person honestly.

Bliss sat back in her seat and munched on some Now and Laters as she went into thought. "I mean, if you think about it, Let. That's all we've been anyway is just friends. Yeah, we sleep, or slept, in the same bed and kissed every now and then, but that was it."

"That's it? Bitch, he a maybe-baby-daddy. Fuck you mean that's it?"

Bliss giggled at her friend, "We only slept together twice. The one time after the cookout and again a few weeks back."

"You serious?" Letty's eyebrows shot up so far, Bliss thought that they were a permanent part of her hairline. "How you sleep next to that fine specimen every night and not sleep with him?"

"It's not like that with Junior. I don't know. We just have a different bond I guess. He's like the calm to my crazy. He knows how to handle me when I'm going through it with the anxiety and shit. He keeps me grounded. I guess you could say that he's my best friend, but that's about it."

"I hear you. I just hope that Junior understands that."

Bliss hoped the same thing. She realized now that Junior was like a safety net for her. He always caught her when she slipped, and fell and she was comfortable. They got along so well, and the chemistry was there. It just wasn't that sizzling, soul connection that she had with Bentley.

The girls went into the mall and shopped for the majority of the early afternoon, and Esa found a cute outfit for her date and bought some things for the baby. She couldn't walk past the children's store without taking a peak.

She didn't want to go overboard this time around for fear that she wouldn't get to dress her baby. She wanted to take her time and ease her way back into the swing of being pregnant again.

Bliss was dead tired and ready for a nap after going through most of the stores. Trying to keep up with Letty was a task within itself, and it was intensified carrying bags around.

They grabbed a seat on a bench and people watched while snacking on some pretzels.

"Have you told Carlos and Sin, yet?" Letty asked, squeezing some mustard, out of the packet onto her pretzel.

"Nah. I planned on telling daddy today. I ain't telling Sin ass nothing." Bliss hated how she and her sister had fallen off, but if she got an instinct to stay away, then she had no choice but to fall back until she figured out what was going on. Her daddy always told her to follow her gut.

"I thought you would be excited to tell Sin."

"I was." Bliss scooped her pretzel down into her cheese sauce. "But ever since I told her I was pregnant with Cielo, she had been acting funny, yo. She ain't even come and see me when I lost my baby."

"That's fucked up and fishy, and those are two f's we don't fuck with."

Bliss giggled, "Facts."

They stopped in a couple more stores before finally heading to the car.

"Can you stop by Krispy Kreme, Let?" Bliss asked, after getting settled in her seat.

"Yo ole fat, greedy ass. Didn't you just have two pretzels?" Letty asked, merging the car into traffic.

"It was one-and-a-half. Fuck you very much." Bliss rolled her eyes dramatically.

"Same difference, hoe."

"Yeah, whatever. These donuts ain't for me, though. They for daddy."

"Better be. I'm not getting fat witcho ass this time around."

"Just drive, Benson."

*****

"Daddy?" Bliss called out for her father as she walked through the side door. When she got no response, she went into the kitchen to set up the gift that she got for him.

She placed the box of a dozen glazed donuts on the kitchen counter next to his coffee pot. On the top of the box, she wrote a note that read, '*Eat up Pop-Pop. Mommy doesn't want to be the only one with a belly.*'

Not knowing what time her father would be home, Bliss went upstairs to her old room. Her dad owned a five-level brownstone including the basement. The ground floor housed the dining room, living room, kitchen, and a bathroom. The other three levels all had two bedrooms, a family room, and a bathroom. The floors were like each of their own personal apartment.

Bliss stayed on the second level whenever she was home. She changed the family room into an office for her photography. She had a desk set up with her computer, printer and scanner, along with her three different cameras.

Art was Esa's passion, and she loved taking pictures or "capturing stolen moments" as she called it. Anything with a camera she had a natural hack for; she knew it was her calling. She loved graphic designing as well.

Esa started to send her work in to different magazines, advertising companies, online websites, and anywhere else that she could think of. She wanted to start chasing her dream, and that's exactly what she was about to do.

Bliss could hear the front door opening, so she paused on the design that she was working on to run downstairs. She pulled out her phone and hid around the corner so she could record his reaction.

"What the hell?" he said with confusion etched onto his handsome face. She heard him mumble 'Pop-Pop' before he let out a celebratory yell. "Esa!!"

She made her presence known. "What you screaming for old man?" He turned around swiftly to face her with a big grin plastered on his face. He ran over to her and scooped her up into a bear hug.

His warm and soapy scent massaged her nostrils as he hugged her tightly to him. Tears sprang out of her eyes as she hugged her dad.

"I missed yo ole punk self." Bliss said through laughter and tears.

She missed her dad, and she regretted the time she spent away from him, but that was the stage that she was at, she just had to be by herself to process the loss of her child. Shit, she was still at that stage, but she hadmnj to start dealing with it differently. Whether she wants it to be or not, it's no longer about her anymore.

"I missed you, too, punk." He kissed her forehead before wiping her tears. "Congratulations, baby," he whispered softly.

It was as if his words caused the dam to break open as Carlos watched the tears cascade down his baby girls face. He pulled her in to him and held her tightly as his own tears silently fell down his face. He was glad to have his daughter home. He knew that she had to figure somethings out for herself, and he didn't want to let her go, but he had to.

There were no words to describe losing a child. You never quite function properly after it. It's like a piece of you is always missing, and you never get over it. You just learn how to breathe through it.

It was tough watching her go through and face everything that had been thrown at her head on, but she was making him proud. She still had a ways to go, but she was getting there.

"Thank you, Daddy." Bliss said, after she calmed down and her tears finally ceased.

"No doubt." he said releasing her. He went over to the donuts and read the note again.

Bliss watched as a small smile graced his face before he turned and went downstairs to the basement where his room was located. Stopping the recording, Bliss made her way back to the office.

A little while later, Carlos came upstairs with some donuts. Bliss looked over her shoulder as he approached her desk. "I figured you could use a break and feed my grandbaby."

A smile plastered onto her face as she released a shaky breath. She figured he wouldn't be mad, but she still valued and thought highly of his opinion.

Her mouth was watering for a donut, but she wanted to wait for him before indulging herself. Now that he was home, she and her baby were about to fuck those donuts up.

She wrapped up her project and settled on the couch next to her dad.

"So how you been?" Carlos asked before polishing off his first donut.

"Can I be honest?"

"Have I ever stopped you?"

She shook her head before taking a deep breath. She told her dad everything that had happened. She told him about her and Junior's relationship, her and Bentley's relationship, all of the fights, the arguments, and the maybe-baby-daddies.

Her dad was really her best friend, and she knew he wouldn't judge her. She just needed someone to listen to her.

Once she told him most of the events taking place, she felt a little better. He didn't say much, just listened to her and cracked a few jokes here and there. Once she was completely done, he sat back and said a few words.

"I'mma tell you some real shit, baby girl. You gotta choose who makes you happy. You can't drag them along forever.

That's just going to extend the pain and damage. Make ya choice, stick with it, and whatever comes after that, youse face it together." He paused to demolish another donut before taking a swig of his beer and continuing with his conversation.

"You all got that spark. Youse just be in the same room, and it's like an explosion goes off. You know where you belong, Bliss, you don't need ya OG for that." he chuckled.

They finished their conversation before heading down to the kitchen for another snack.

"Did you tell Sin yet?" Carlos asked, as he placed the popcorn in the microwave.

"No." Bliss held her next comment when she heard heels clicking against the hardwood floor. She looked at her dad with a confused look as the heels clicked closer.

"And what did we not tell her?" Aria spoke up from the kitchen entranceway.

Bliss rolled her eyes at the sight of her mother before looking over to her father. "What is she doing here?"

"I came here to talk with ya father."

"Well, you'se have fun. I'll call you later, Daddy." Bliss hopped down from her spot on top of the kitchen counter. Her energy completely depleted whenever her mother was around.

"Always running for the hills whenever ya mother comes around huh?" Aria sat down at the table.

"Pretty much." *Don't feed into it, Bliss. Just ignore her and leave. Don't feed into it,* Bliss coached herself silently. As of late, it

170

didn't take much to set Bliss' temper off. She was working on keeping it under control, however, her tolerance for bullshit had been zero to none. On top of that, her hormones had been all over the place since being pregnant, so it really didn't take much to set her off.

"Typical."

"You know what?" Bliss felt her control slipping.

"Tell me what's on your mind, Pumpkin." Aria said, sarcastically, as she smirked.

Bliss slammed her hands down on the kitchen table. "You're such a condescending little bit-"

"That's enough!" Carlos' voice boomed off of the kitchen walls, silencing the petty argument once and for all. "Got damn, man! Why every time we get together, there always has to be arguing and shit. I'm sick of it."

"Man, I don't have time for this shit." Bliss said, walking towards the small hallway that led to the front door. She had better shit to do than to sit around playing tit-for-tat with her crazy ass mother.

"Sit down, Bliss."

"Oh let her go Carlos." Aria waved her hand dismissively. "She don't have to be around me. Ain't hurting my feelings none. I'm used to seeing the door slam whenever we're together."

Bliss grabbed her jacket out of the hall closet before walking to her father. She placed a quick peck on his cheek.

"I'll see you later, Daddy." And with that, she left out of the house leaving the negative energy there with them.

# Chapter Thirteen

Bliss gave herself a once over in her full-length mirror. She looked good in a pair of ripped skinny jeans, a black tank top, and a red and black flower kimono. A pair of red hoop earrings donned her lobes, and a pair of black, chunky heel boots blessed her feet. She was thankful that they were comfortable shoes.

It was almost time for her first official date with Bentley, and Esa was a little nervous but excited overall. They had been texting throughout the day, talking shit and flirting back and forth. Bliss had been asking all day where he was taking her, but he would not spill.

"Damn, baby, you looking good in them jeans." Bliss laughed at her crazy best friend. Letty smacked Esa on her ass before plopping down onto the bed. "Bent bitch ass better be glad that I like him."

"Why you say that?"

"Cause, I don't have shit to do tonight."

"I'm coming back tonight, Let. You all in yo bag like you walking me down the aisle or some shit." Bliss joked.

"Might as well be. And I know for a fact that ya ass not coming back."

"How you figure?"

"If it were me. My ass would be laid up under his fine ass somewhere. Plus, you my best friend, so I know you got it in you, witcho two maybe-baby-daddies having ass."

Bliss smirked while finishing her last touch of eyeliner. "Shut up, hoe. I thought that you and Riq had a Netflix date later?"

"This nigga canceled on me. Said some shit popped off at one of the houses."

Bliss' eyebrows rose. "Word?"

"Hell, yeah, so he said we can get up later on tonight once he handles it or whatever." Letty said rolling her eyes.

"Well, that fucking blows." Bliss was in the middle of applying Vaseline to her lips when she abruptly stopped and faced Letty. "You want me to cancel?"

"You better bring ya ass, Juice."

Bliss' heart flipped when the deep baritone rang out from down the hall. Her eyes widened as she looked at Letty. "You could've told me that he was here, hoe." Bliss scolded.

Letty rolled her eyes. "He can wait. His ass early any damn way."

"You're cute when you get jealous." Bliss giggled. She pulled Letty up off of the bed before backing up. "So, how do I look?"

"Wonderful darling. Fresh off of the runway."

Just then Bent poked his head into the room. "Yo punk ass still aint ready?"

"Shut up," she said before smiling. "Impatient ass."

"Just hurry yo slow, turtle moving ass up." he smirked, before turning and walking back up the hallway.

"Just go. Leave me by my lonesome here all night."

"I love you." Bliss smiled at her friend, as she walked down the hall to an impatient Bentley. Her smile widened when she stopped right in front in him.

She drunk him in with her eyes. She took in the way his broad shoulders filled out his black and white checkered button down shirt. The black toboggan that he had on over his dreads matched perfectly. The classic wheat-colored Timb's that he rocked brought everything together perfectly. The only jewelry that he had on was his all-black watch, his two gold chains that he always wore, and some black gold studs. The simple look, looked good on him.

He smirked down at her, "What's up, Ma?" He kissed her forehead before grabbing her hand and pulling her into him.

"Hi," she said wrapping her arms around his neck. He pecked her lips and squeezed her tighter into him. Bliss exhaled and let the tension that was in her body go. She planned on enjoying herself tonight.

"See you later, Let." Bliss said unlocking the door.

"Alright. Keep ya hands to yourself, Bentley. I don't mind cutting a nigga."

"I got you, even though I ain't scared of yo little ass." He laughed.

"Yeah, whatever. Just remember what I said, nigga."
He nodded before following Bliss out of the door.

"Don't wait up. Lock The door." he said over his
shoulder before the door slammed shut behind him.

*****

"Man, whatever. I whipped that ass, and you know it."

"Boy, bye. You was choking on the cloud of dust when
I pulled off." Bliss responded, crunching into a salty tortilla
chip. She moaned as the saltiness coated her tongue. Her baby
was making her crave salty and sweet. If it wasn't one, it was
the other.

"Yeah, I hear you." Bent took a drink of the water that
the waitress had just sat down in front of him.

Bentley surprised Bliss by renting out her favorite go-
kart race track. For the last couple of hours, Bliss and Bent
raced, crashed, and laughed their way around the track.

Now they were looking over menus at a Mexican
restaurant. They were seated in a cozy booth towards the back
of the restaurant. Bent liked to sit where he could see
practically every inch of the restaurant.

"I still beat that ass, though. I don't care what you say,
Miss Esa." Bent laughed out loud when Bliss threw her half-
eaten tortilla chip at him.

Bliss laughed when he picked the chip up from his lap
and tossed it into his mouth. "Greedy". She pouted when he
snatched her next chip out of her hand. "I wanted that."

They ordered their food before falling into conversation. Bliss' cheeks were hurting, along with her stomach, from laughing and smiling so much. She didn't know what to expect, but she was glad that she gave him a second chance.

Bliss did her happy, fat dance, as the waitress placed her shrimp and chicken tacos, with the extra sides of queso and salsa, down in front of her.

Bentley chuckled as he watched her dive in. Esa did not have any shame in her game when it came to eating. She would snack all day, but could keep up and get down and dirty with the best of them. Especially, if she had a craving.

They were making small talk and laughing when Bliss noticed that the smile fell off of Bentley's face.

"What's the matter?" she asked him with concern lacing her tone.

"I'll be right back." He slid out of the booth before she had the chance to respond.

The waitress came back over to the table, distracting Bliss from following Bentley with her eyes.

By the time Bent made it back to the table a few minutes later, Bliss had all of their food packed and ready to go. She was standing in front of the table with her jacket on and her bag on her shoulder.

"Somebody ready to go, huh?" He ended his walk in front of her.

"I ain't know if we had to run up outta here by the way you hopped up from the table."

"My bad, Juice. I aint mean to scare you."

"I'm not scared. I was just getting ready for any event in case some shit popped off."

He laughed, "You wasn't playing no games. Got the food packed and ready to go and shit." he laughed again, "You wasn't leaving that, huh?"

"Hell no. Shit, the way I look at it, that's snack's for later. You gone learn I don't play about my food."

"Snack is life I see."

"Dead ass. My snack game on 1,000." She paused before smiling, as she rubbed her stomach. She always had a little pudge around her stomach, but now it was a little more defined. She mainly carried her pregnancy in her hips and ass. "Especially, with my mini; I stay hungry."

Bliss watched as Bent licked his lips before pulling them into a smile. She wanted to reach up and kiss the life out of him, but she composed herself instead and settled for a small smile.

"Come on, Ma, let's go."

*****

"Get the fuck outta here." Bentley looked over to Bliss like she had grown four heads. "You've never seen *Paid in Full*?"

They were at Bentley's house, stretched out on his couch together, arguing over which movie to watch. Bent had a huge flat screen projector mounted on the wall in his living room. He also had a whole collection of movies to watch on it.

"How you from New York and never seen it?" Bentley asked continuing his rant.

"I've seen *Juice*." she shrugged nonchalantly.

"You get points, but it ain't the same, so we watching *Paid in Full*."

"That's fine." Bliss ghosted her fingers over his scalp. "Can I grease your scalp?"

"Hell yeah, my shit need some TLC." Bentley loved when his hair was played with. It had been so long since he allowed someone other than his hairdresser to lay hands on his crown. His hair was important to him, so he didn't allow just anybody in it.

"Get my bag for me, please." Once she had her bag, she pulled out a small glass jar.

"What's that?" he asked looking at the jar sideways.

"Coconut oil."

"Fuck is that?" Bent asked scrunching up his face.

"Don't worry 'bout it. Just sit yo tall ass on the floor." He shot her a warning look. "Please?" she added smiling.

She adjusted some pillows on the couch so that she could sit on them and see the top of his head. After putting the movie on, Bent got settled and laid his head back on her lap.

She looked down and saw that he was staring up at her. She kissed his forehead before bending over and kissing his lips. Esa loved the feeling that she got whenever he was around. He held her head there before kissing her again. "Don't fuck my shit up either, Juice. I'm not playing."

"Trust me. This is what I does." She pecked his lips again before righting herself and starting on his hair.

After blessing his scalp with the coconut oil, she decided to braid his dreads back into two braids. The movie ended just as Bliss was finishing her last braid.

"They didn't have to do my nigga Mitch like that, though." Bliss said, stretching.

"Facts! Ole bitch ass, Rico." Bent agreed. He picked her up off of the couch, his hands glued to her soft, plump ass.

"I had fun tonight." Bliss said, wrapping her hands around his neck, careful not to get any of the excess oil from her hands on his clothes. Even though he stripped out of the button down he had on and into just his black undershirt, she still did not want to mess it up.

Bent raised his eyebrows. "Oh, really?"

She bit her lip as she nodded her head. "Mhm." She ran her hands over his beard, wiping the excess oil on his soft, but course facial hair. Bentley was a proud member of the beard gang, and Bliss loved every inch of it.

"Good." He kissed her lips. "You gone be my girl, now?"

Her hands paused as she looked him in his eyes. He could see the hesitation in her eyes. "I don't know, Bentley."

Irritation flashed through him, but he kept it at bay. He did fuck up royally with her, so he knew that he had to keep his patience topped off to a low level.

"I fucked up the first time around with you. I'm not about to allow that shit to pop off again." He grabbed her chin to make sure she was looking into his eyes. "You already mine, Bliss. I'm just waiting for you to realize that shit."

Bent felt his blood began to boil with her next words.

"I gotta think about Juni-"

"What about him?" he cut her off with a frown on his face. His tone indignant.

"He deserves to be taken into consideration, too, Bent." She watched as he clenched and unclenched his jaw.

"June don't have nothing to do with you and me." He placed her down on the floor. "Stop acting like you not feeling me. Like you don't feel this." He waved his hand in between them. "I know you want this shit just as much as I do. Fuck him at this point, man. Dead ass."

She dropped her eyes from his intense gaze. "What if my baby not yours?"

"Look at me, Bliss." He waited until she followed instructions. "They gonna be mine regardless, because they are a part of you. I don't care who the biological father is. Anything that's a part of you is automatically a part of me. We'll deal with that when it gets here, baby girl."

He sat down on the couch with her straddling his lap. He wiped the tears that started to fall down her red cheeks. "I want you, Juice. Been wanting yo little ass since you stepped on my Jays." He cracked a smile when she smacked her teeth.

"Oh, whatever! You stepped all on my shit with yo damn tug boats." she giggled through her tears.

"Damn, just coming at the kid top like that?"

She nodded her head curtly while trying to contain her smile. "Damn, right."

He put his hands in her hair before meeting her lips with his own in a heated kiss, and she moaned at the unexpected pleasure.

Her arms found their way around his neck as he kissed the soul out of her. He was pouring everything into that kiss … his need, want, and hunger for her. He craved her, not only mentally and physically, but emotionally as well. He needed her by his side just as bad as she wanted to be there.

Every feeling. Every emotion. Every thought that she buried deeply when she cut Bent off, came rushing back at once.

Each lick, nibble, and bite that Bent deliciously delivered to her lips, Bliss felt her guard crumble a little more.

Esa was scared; hell, she was petrified of getting hurt. As much as she wanted to run as far away as possible to avoid giving in, she knew she couldn't fight the feelings that she was developing for him.

She wasn't so sure if she wanted to anymore. It became clear to her that that was where she wanted to be.

Bentley broke their kiss apart before grabbing her chin as he placed a few pecks on her moist lips. "So you going to ride with ya nigga or not?"

She fixed her face and pretended to think hard for a few seconds before finally speaking. "Till the wheels fall off."

The smile that made its way across Bentley's face as she spoke warmed Bliss to her core, and she knew that she was making the right decision.

"And even then, I got the spare on deck." he said, smacking her ass before gripping it and pulling her closer to him.

\*\*\*\*\*

*"You're so beautiful, give the world a show. Go up, down, up, down, up, down."*

Ignoring the insistent noise, Bliss shut her eyes tighter and snuggled closer to the warmth of Bentley. He turned over on his side before he wrapped his arm around her and pulled her closer to him.

"Let me find out you cheating on me already." Bent's voice was full of sleep, causing it to be deep and husky, as it vibrated throughout the dark room.

"Hmmm?" Bliss said still sleeping.

"That's the third time somebody called you. It's three am."

Bliss popped her head up. "Somebody called me?" Bent sat them up and grabbed her phone off of the nightstand. He handed it to her before laying back down.

"Thank you." She mumbled before checking her notifications. She was half- asleep, squinting at her bright phone trying to read her text messages. It was proving to be a harder task through her sleep-encrusted eyelashes.

"What the hell is going on?"

"What's up, Juice?" Bent asked. He sat up and looked at her, now on high alert.

She had one finger held up, signaling for him to give her one moment. He was about to start being petty by fucking with her neck, but the serious facial expression halted his movements.

Bliss hopped off of the bed and put her jeans back on. "Fuck she at, yo?" She paused as she waited on a response on the other end of the line. "I'm on my way."

She hung up before quickly padding across the floor into Bent's closet.

"What's going on, Esa?" He heard her rummaging around before she came out with one of his hoodies on.

"Tyriq and Letty got into this big fight, I guess. He said he's worried about her." She put her hair up in a bun and walked into the bathroom.

"He just hit me up. This shit is serious." Bent said, reading over the 911 text that Riq sent him.

"Hell, yeah." Bliss agreed. "Normally, she would have been blowing me up screaming at the top of her lungs. She didn't even check-in earlier, which was very weird." Bent threw some clothes on before joining her in the master bathroom. "What Tyriq say?"

Bent shrugged, "He sent a text saying to hit him back."

Bliss nodded. "I'm ready. You have to carry me though, my Timb's are in the car." She hopped on the bed before jumping on his back.

"They got me fucked up." Bliss began to rant through a yawn. "Do they not know what time it is? Don't they know not to wake a sleeping, pregnant woman." She paused to nuzzle her forehead against his neck. "Especially one that's an insomniac. Let there be a single hair out of place on Letty head, and I'm punching Riq right between his eyes." she continued her venting as they made their way to the car.

"Let me ask you something. How are you going to reach up that high?" Bentley asked.

"How you get that scar on your forehead?"

Bentley fell out in laughter. "Damn, it's like that?" Bliss just smirked as she hopped in the truck.

Pulling up to Tyriq's house, Bliss scrunched her face in confusion.

She was expecting blood, bullet casings, and weave tracks to be sprayed all over the yard. She didn't see anything, and the feeling of dread threatened to creep up her spine. *Odd,* she thought to herself.

She was out of the car and in the house in the blink of an eye, with Bent right behind her.

"Letty?!"

# Chapter Fourteen

Letty sighed and rolled off of her stomach onto her back. "I need to get out of this house." She was tired of scrolling through Instagram and watching people have fun on Snap Chat.

Letty was really a loner, who did not like to be alone. She didn't fuck with too many people, and she liked her space, but on the same hand, she hated sleeping alone and being in her apartment by herself for long periods of time. She would begin to feel restless.

In an attempt to relax, Letty decided to soak in her tub, so she ran a hot bath and placed her 'Honey Bee' bath bomb in the steaming hot water. Then she lit some candles and rolled a couple of blunts.

Finding the right playlist, she grabbed her blunts and a tall glass of wine before sliding into the tub and letting the scented, hot water consume her.

After draining the water from her bath, Letty turned on the shower and washed her body. She liked soaking just to relax, but she wouldn't feel clean until she took a shower.

She called Tyriq and didn't get an answer. She knew he was probably still trying to handle whatever situation was going on, so she let him be for now. She would just see him out at their house later on tonight.

It was Saturday, and whenever Tyriq had to work late, Letty would buy them dinner and greet him when he walked through the door. Not only would his plate be hot and ready, but she would have a blunt freshly lit, a cold glass of Henny, and her pussy wet and all ready to go on a silver platter.

Letty loved her man and showed it with her actions. She wasn't the lovey dovey type of girlfriend that clung to you and professed their love every three seconds; she was more in the lines of 'what's understood, doesn't have to be explained'.

Tyriq knew she loved him, and she knew he loved her, too, and that was what was important.

She wasn't going to keep a tight leash on her man, as long as he didn't give her a reason to and if he did give her a reason to, she would beat his ass and whoever he was fucking.

There were a few bitches back in the day that she had to pistol whip, but nothing ever too serious. Letty didn't know whether or not it was because Tyriq did a wonderful job of keeping them at bay, but for the most part, the bitches kept their distance.

Tyriq knew that Letty was certified crazy. She should probably have some papers somewhere or be documented on somebody's paperwork but she ain't have time for all of that. Life was too short.

She dressed casually in an oversized, long-sleeved 'NY' t-shirt and a pair of ripped skinny jeans. A pair of Air Max 90's donned her pretty, manicured feet.

Letty didn't have any plans other than to go and get some food, and after that, it was time to head straight to their crib and watch a movie until daddy came home and gave her that dope dick she had been craving all day.

Letty wanted some Jamaican food but missed the carry-out so she decided to get her favorite wings from this bar in her neighborhood called Lady's. The food was amazing, the drinks were strong, and it wasn't that expensive, so to say the least, Letty was a known face in the bar.

"Hey, Letty!" the bartender, Jennifer, said as Letty hopped on the barstool.

If Letty wasn't strictly dickly, she would have been snatched Jennifer's sexy ass up. Jen was 5'7 with thick hips, a plump ass, and thick, voluptuous thighs. Her stomach was slim, minus the little pudge that never budged no matter how hard she worked to get rid of it.

If Letty didn't know any better, she would have thought that Jen was black based off of her shape and her actions. On top of her being sin in heels, Jen was the coolest white person that Letty had ever known.

Letty could consider Jen a friend, but she didn't do those. If you didn't fuck with Letty way back when, then you definitely did not fuck with her now.

"Hey, Jen" Letty smiled politely. She was sociable, but not too much. She preferred to sit back and watch her surroundings. "Can I have twenty-five wings with the sweet and spicy Asian sauce. And a large order of fries?"

"Yeah, no problem. Anything else?"

"A Henny with a dab of ginger ale please? You know how I like it." She flashed Jen a small smile.

"I got ya." Jennifer winked before making Letty's drink and sitting it down in front of her.

"That's a strong drink." A deep, husky, and slightly accented voice said from beside Letty. She didn't know what kind of accent it was, but what she did know was that it had her panties soaked to capacity.

She turned to look over her shoulder and was met by one of the sexiest men she had ever seen in her life, which was hard for her to believe, because he wasn't exactly her favorite flavor of ice cream. She never really could get with the swirl, but she never discriminated.

Surprisingly, her mouth was watering at the thought of getting a taste of him. He reminded her of the sexy British singer, Zayn Malik. He even sounded like him a little bit, except on top of the other accent, there was a strong NY accent as well. They blended well and made this man sound like the pearly gates to heaven.

"I'm a big girl." She flashed a side smile at him as his eyes slowly drank in her body from head to toe. From the small smile that appeared on his face, she could tell that he appreciated what he saw, so she returned the favor and was thoroughly impressed.

This man had to have been handcrafted by God himself. His sun-kissed, vanilla skin served as the easel that his narrow nose, plump bottom lip, and light brown eyes were painted on. The way that his short and stubby beard highlighted his chiseled jaw line made her clutch her pearls like they were about to become extinct.

She looked away before she got carried away. The way his all black, leather lettermen jacket hung on his broad shoulders was calling out to her. How it perfectly displayed his crisp white V-neck and gold chain did something to her. Her knees weakened as his Gucci cologne invaded her nostrils, making her thank God that she was already sitting.

Slowly, she sipped on her drink before turning her attention to one of the many flat screen TVs in the bar. Her phone buzzed in her lap pulling her attention away from ESPN.

It was a message from Tyriq, but before she could unlock her phone, an extended, tattooed hand appeared in her line of vision.

She looked up and was met with her new comrades pretty, brown eyes.

"I'm Bishop." His eyes crinkled as his lips pulled back into a smile revealing a perfectly white smile and a blinged out bottom grill. She wasn't really a fan of grills, but she had to admit, he made them shit's sexy.

*Who is this white boy that got me tripping like this?* Letty thought to herself.

She placed her small hand into his large one. "I'm Letty." He squeezed her hand gently before bringing it to his lips. Goosebumps broke out all over her arm when his lips connected to her flesh.

"It's a pleasure to meet you, Letty." His intense gaze mixed with his dazzling smile had Letty stunned quiet. It was like her mouth and brain weren't meshing, and her words got lost somewhere.

His phone went off on the counter causing the spell that they were just under to be broken. She pulled her hand back quickly before placing it in her lap.

"Food's almost up, Letty. Want the usual sauces?" Jennifer spoke up from the kitchen door causing Letty to look up.

"Yeah, that's fine. Thank you."

"Yeah. I'm on my way." Letty heard Bishop end his call.

"Sorry about that." he smiled, nervously at the beautiful woman in front of him. She turned to smile at him, and he knew that he had to see her again. It was something about her eyes that drew him in. He could see something in them.

"I have to go and handle something. Are you going to be here for a while?" He watched as Jennifer came out with two bags of food and handed them to Letty, thus answering his question. He discreetly caught Jennifer's attention and motioned for her to put the food on his tab.

"Actually, this is me." Letty said, eyeing the food hungrily before checking over everything to make sure it was exactly how she ordered it. She dug in her purse and pulled out some cash. "How much?"

"It's already taken care of." Letty looked up at Jennifer shocked. Jennifer nodded her head to the side motioning to Bishop, before winking and walking away.

Catching on, Letty looked over to Bishop. "You didn't have to do that." She didn't know how to feel about his gesture. She took pride in being independent. Letty worked hard for her money and enjoyed spending it. She didn't need to depend on anyone, besides her damn self, for anything because that was all she had in the end.

"I don't do anything that I don't want to do." He slid off of his stool and stepped closer to her while placing his hand on the back of her neck. He slowly caressed his thumb back and forth across her smooth, coffee skin. "I have to go now, beautiful, but I will be in touch." He kissed her cheek softly before disappearing into the crowd of patrons.

Letty was looking in the direction after Bishop like a deer caught in head lights; she was stuck. Shaking her head, she snapped out of whatever spell Bishop had her under.

*What the hell was that?* she thought to herself trying to get her life all the way together.

Gathering her items, she slid Jennifer the twenty dollar bill she had in her hand before retreating from the bar.

\*\*\*\*\*

*"I don't wanna die too young, too young. I've been grindin' way too long."*

Singing along to "Too Young" by Post Malone, Letty was cruising down the street that Tyriq's house was on. She pulled into the driveway and turned up the music so that she could sing along to her part as loud as she wanted to. She could never get out of the car when her song was on.

"That was my shit." she giggled to herself as she climbed out of the truck. Still humming along to the beat in her head, she grabbed her bags and the food out of the back seat. She couldn't wait to get in the house and fuck them wings up.

Letty had her key out and almost in the key hole when the door swung open. She jumped back as her eyes registered what was going on. The food and bags that were in her hand fell to the floor as her mind tried to process her boyfriend wrapped around another woman.

In the house that he, for all intents and purposes, shared with her … his girlfriend.

"Letty? Wh-what are you doing here?" Tyriq asked, surprised to see his girl there at the house. He sent her a text earlier saying that he wanted to move their Netflix date location to her apartment.

He dropped his arm from around the girl so quick, you would have thought that she was crawling in spiders.

"Baby, who's this?" the girl asked with her face scrunched up.

Tyriq rolled his eyes at the girl in front of him. He was hoping she would stay quiet and let him do the talking so that they both could leave with no bullet wounds or even better … alive.

Letty looked at him with a flash of pain evident in her eyes, before it morphed into anger. "You dead ass?" she asked him in disbelief. "You have to be fucking kidding me, Tyriq!"

*Baby who's this?* Letty repeated the phrase over and over in her head as her mind tried to place the puzzle pieces together. She knew Tyriq wasn't this fucking stupid. After all they had been through together, this was what he pulled next?

From taking bullets for one another to shooting motherfuckas together, you name it, they've done it.

She was his Bonnie in her truest form.

She gave him whatever the fuck he wanted, when he wanted it, however he wanted it, and this was the bullshit that he pulled.

"Baby?" Letty spit the word out with venom dripping heavily from each syllable. "So this ya bitch?"

"Excuse me?" The girl huffed, "I don't know who you are-"

*SMACK!*

Letty openhandedly smacked the girl. "Bitch, you in my house! You don't get to talk to me. I will fucking kill you." She mushed the girl in the head with her hand. "I don't know who he let you think you are, but you better get up to speed with who the fuck I am. Don't ever address me, bitch. Remember that."

"A'ight look; you can't just be smacking her and shit, Letty."

She looked at Tyriq baffled. "So you defending bitches now?" What the hell was going on? When Letty found out Tyriq was cheating on her the last couple of times, she went off on Tyriq and beat the girls up.

Tyriq never intervened for the simple fact that it was better them than him. He also knew Letty was going to fuck the broads up anyway, because that was how she was. She was fiercely loyal, but if you disrespected her in any way, she would let it be known.

That was why it was crazy to her that he would defend the broad. That meant it wasn't just some random fling or casual hook-up. He cared for the girl, or at least cared enough to stop the ass whooping that was surely set to come her way.

"Let me talk to you, Letty." Tyriq said reaching for her arm. She snatched away from him, and he held his arms up in surrender. He knew how she was and didn't want to upset her more than she already was. He was trying to avoid all of the dramatics he knew was to come.

Tyriq was losing control of the situation quickly, and he couldn't afford for that to happen. He needed to tell her something before it got out there and it was too late.

"I can't believe you just hit me!" the girl said holding the side of her face.

The little bit of patience Letty did have went right out of the window at the annoying sound of that girl's voice.

Letty lunged forward and grabbed the girl by her hair. She was able to land two punches against the girl's skull before Tyriq pulled her away.

"Got damn it, Letty! Sit yo ass down! You can't be fighting her while she carrying my son!" He pushed her away so hard that she stumbled before gaining her balance.

*Son?* Letty ran the phrase over and over in her mind. *Carrying my son.*

For the first time, Letty took in the girl standing before her. Her eyes zoomed in on the girls round, protruding belly.

She felt like the wind had been knocked right out of her sails as the breath left her body. She locked eyes with Tyriq to see if he was serious.

Tears stung her eyes as she realized that he was.

He reached out for her arm, and she lost it. "Don't fucking touch me!" She started to push and hit him as her anger bubbled out. "After everything Riq?"

"A'ight, man, stop fucking putting ya hands on me, Letisha." Tyriq was getting angrier and angrier by the second. This wasn't how this was supposed to happen. This wasn't how he planned how to tell her. "I fucked up yo!"

"You fucking right!" She couldn't stop the rage that she felt pouring out of her as she kept hitting him. She wanted to hurt him as much as she was hurting right now.

Tyriq back handed her, and she flew into the end table by the entrance of the house. The items on the table went flying everywhere. "Got damn it, Letty! Fuck man!" He stormed out of the front door.

Rubbing her cheek, Letty spit out the blood in her mouth before getting up off of the floor. She grabbed her purse and went upstairs to the master bedroom. She locked the door and went straight into the closet.

She refused to cry. She refused to drop another fucking tear over this nigga. *Fuck him.*

Letty could feel herself shutting down. She didn't feel any emotion right now, except for the burning rage that was pulsating through her body. Every ounce of sadness was gone; the hurt and betrayal she felt all morphed into anger. She fucking hated him.

How could he do this to the woman he called his rib? The woman that *he* said that he prayed for. How could you call her the answer to your prayers and then turn around and disrespect her? What the fuck kind of love is that?

She came from a fucked up past of not having her parents, being bounced around from foster home to foster home, and being raped for the majority of her adolescent life.

Not having anybody to love you or show you how to love, you're forced to pick a few things up along the way to teach yourself. She may not know everything about it, but one thing Letty knew for sure, was that this wasn't love. It just couldn't be.

"Letty?" she heard Tyriq sigh deeply as he tried to open the door, only to realize that it was locked. "Baby, let me in the room. I'm sorry."

She ignored him as she gathered the clothes that she had at that house.

They each had their own apartments, but they brought this house together last year. This was their weekend house where they came to spend time together. This was their escape from the hectic lives that they lived.

After his pleas had fallen on deaf ears, Tyriq began to incessantly bang on the door. She was just praying that the door did not break down, because she was really trying not to shoot his ass. However, he was stomping on that last button of sanity that she had.

Letty grabbed a pre-rolled blunt from the dresser, which was where their smoke stash was, before grabbing her gun that was tucked right next to the weed. She backed away from the door and aimed her gun towards it.

**BANG!**

The door flew off the hinges, revealing a very angry Tyriq on the other side of it. If it were under different circumstances, she probably would have laughed and cracked a joke, but she felt nothing.

"I'm just tryna talk to you, Letty."

She said nothing as she pulled on the blunt. "Don't come near me, Tyriq. Just go back with ya baby mother. By the time you get back, I'll be gone."

He smacked his teeth, "You not going anywhere, man." He stepped towards her at the same time he felt a bullet whiz by his head. "You dead ass right now, yo? You almost shot me!"

She smirked. "Now you know better than that, baby. I always hit my mark."

"Baby, I-" Tyriq began.

"My name is Letisha to you, nigga. Not Letty. Not Let. It's definitely not Baby! From this moment on, Tyriq," She paused and looked him square in the eye. "I don't want anything to do with you. Just let me get my shit and leave."

"Man, fuck that." he said bum rushing her and knocking the gun out of her hand. "We gonna talk about this." he said, wrapping his arms around her so that she couldn't get out of his grasp.

"Why you gotta be so fucking difficult?! You did this shit, Tyriq. You got that bitch pregnant, not me, so let me go."

"You just gonna give up on us like that? You ready to quit? I thought we was in this thing forever. No matter what life threw at us?"

"Don't flip this shit on me. You took that option away from me." she said, as she struggled against his hold.

"I let you do whatever the fuck you wanted to, man. I never nagged you; I don't breathe down ya neck. All I ever asked was for you not bring home no fucking STD's, no ratchet hoes, and No. Fucking. Babies! Who the fuck knows what else you brought back to me, nigga. Fucking these bitches raw and shit.

"That obviously means that you don't give no fucks about Letty. Fucking these hoes raw and then come back home dicking me down and shit. Nigga, fuck you! Now, get off of me." She stomped on his barefoot with the heel of her sneaker before head butting him in the nose.

"Arrrgh!" Screaming out in agony, Tyriq dropped the gun and reached for his nose. "Fucking psychotic ass bitch" he said, applying pressure to his nose to stop the bleeding.

Bending down, Letty picked up her gun and the blunt that he made her drop. "But you knew that from the moment you met me. Fuck out my face."

Aiming the gun at Tyriq, Letty watched as Tyriq put his hands up slowly.

"Letisha, put the gun down so that we can talk."

"I don't want to hear anything that you have to say, Tyriq."

"Why you doing me like that, Ma?"

"You brought that bitch in my house. You got this bitch in here talking disrespectfully to me like my name not on this shit, too. You at least could have been a man and checked her ass."

"Stop insulting me."

"Insulting you?" Letty chuckled dejectedly. "You want me to stop insulting you?" she chuckled again. "When I took that bullet that was targeted for you and miscarried our baby, we knew a long time ago that we wouldn't be able to have children. And now? You in my face telling me that you got some bitch pregnant, yet somehow you want me to stop insulting you?" She looked at him with a baffled expression pinched on her face.

"How far along is the bitch?" Letty told herself that she didn't want to know, but she was lying to herself.

"Seven." Tyriq said.

"Seven, what? Seven days? Weeks? How far along is the bitch Tyriq?"

"Cassie is seven months pregnant." Tyriq said hanging his head low.

"Are you fucking kidding me right now, Tyriq?" Letty continued before shaking her head in disbelief. "Just go."

Letty couldn't even fathom a sentence to even begin to try to express how she felt.

She just knew that she couldn't be with him, near him or even in the same vicinity as him.

"Let, I'm-" he began to say to her.

"Tyriq." She said his name through clenched teeth. She really didn't have the energy to be here right now. She just wanted him to leave her alone and let her leave.

Letty watched as he backed out of the room defeated. She held her breath until she heard the front door slam shut.

Releasing a breath, Letty fell to her knees as the weight of the situation hit her like a ton of bricks.

*A baby?* The tears burned the back of her eyes and blurred her vision before finally falling free.

She didn't move from her spot on the floor as she laid there and cried her eyes out.

*****

"Letty?" Bliss said, softly, stroking Letty's hair. "Come on, baby, get up. I'mma take you home."

Letty nodded before getting up and hugging her best friend. She couldn't find the strength to talk. There were no words to describe the pain that she felt. Tyriq was the first man she had ever loved, and he most definitely would be the last.

*Fuck Love and fuck him.*

# Chapter Fifteen

"Bitch, get up!" Bliss said, bursting through Letty's bedroom door. It had been weeks since Tyriq and Letty's breakup, and Letty was still taking it rather hard. She barely moved out of her bed.

She went to work just enough not to get fired. She showered just enough not to stink, and she ate just enough not to starve. That's all Letty had the energy and the will to do.

Other than that, she was just existing, and her best friend was at her wits end with it. She loved Letty, but it was time for her to get her shit together.

Letty was about to fly off of the handle from the rude intrusion until the delicious smell of food blessed her nostrils.

"Mhm, I dare you to say something smart, nigga." Bliss said, knowingly. She handed Letty the plate of home fries, eggs, and home-made empanadas.

Letty's stomach grumbled before she quickly took a bite. "What time is it?"

Bliss handed her a cup of Cran-Apple juice before answering. "six-thirty."

Letty choked on the gulp of juice that she had just taken. "In the morning?"

"Yeah." Bliss answered nonchalantly. She barked out a laugh when Letty looked at her like she had lost her mind. "I had a craving, yo. Don't judge me."

"No judgment." Letty bit into the crispy empanada, "I'm not gone lie. These shits is banging. Bliss smiled, as she watched her friend.

After a few moments, she spoke up. "It's time to get up, Let."

"Bitch, it's the ass crack of dawn. I'm taking my black ass back to sleep." Letty responded before shoveling a forkful of potatoes in her mouth.

"No dummy. It's time to get up out of this house. I know you got knocked down with this fuckery, but a boss always holds her head high. Fuck that nigga."

Letty took offense quickly, "Bitch, ain't nobody say nothing after you went through ya shit when you and that nigga split."

"I let you have your time. It's been going on three months, Ma. You have to get up some time and start being you again. You was Letty before that, and you gone be Letty after that nigga. And let me tell you something else. I was mourning my child, not being done with that nigga. Don't ever get that shit confused, Letisha." Bliss felt some type of way about how Letty came for her, but she reigned in her attitude.

After a moment in silence, Bliss spoke up. "Here." She slid Letty a wad of cash across the bed. "Go see Sandra and Leah; get them hair and nails done."

"I got my own money, Bliss."

"Did I ask you that?" Letty didn't respond, as she continued to eat her food. It was a moot point to argue with Bliss. "Eat up, my love. I'm going to the park with Bent. I'll be back later."

"Thanks for brunch." Letty smirked.

"Welcome. There's more on the counter." Bliss was halfway out of the door, when she suddenly remembered something else. "Oh. Here, boo." She handed Let a rolled blunt, then shrugged when Letty looked at her weird.

"I miss rolling up." she sighed. "Plus, your insomniac ass is not gone let it go to waste. I'll see you later."

After finishing off her first plate, Letty smoked the gifted blunt that Bliss gave her before polishing off a second plate. She cocooned herself in her blankets as her thoughts consumed her.

She decided that Bliss was right. It was time to get up off of her ass and hit the pavement hard. First thing on her agenda was going to get her wig snatched to the hair gods. Today was about her and the return of Letty.

\*\*\*\*\*

"Hey, Pop!" Bliss said, cheerfully, as she made her way into the kitchen in her father's house. She and Bentley stopped by her dad's so that she could formally introduce them. The first time they met was under worse circumstances.

"Hola, Mami." Carlos kissed Bliss on her cheek before directing his attention to Bentley. "What's up, young man?"

"How you doing?" Bentley stretched his hand out in greeting. "I'm Bentley."

"Carlos." After shaking hands, the men nodded at each other before sitting down at the kitchen table. "How was the park this morning? Did you get some good shots?" Carlos directed his question to Bliss.

"Yeah, I did. It's kind of gloomy out there, so the pictures came out awesome."

"Good. You know walking will help with the baby. Youse keep walking every day like you do, and that baby will walk right out."

Bliss rose her eyebrows. "Oh, really?"

"Yeah. I seen it with ya mother. I swear, Sin slid right out." he chuckled before clearing his throat. "I invited ya mother over."

Bliss involuntarily smacked her teeth as the smile faded off of her face. "For what?"

"That's ya mother, Bliss. Like it or not."

"I don't get why you feel the need to keep forcing this shit between us. It's not happening and probably never will."

"Watch ya mouth." Carlos gave Bliss a warning look before continuing. "She's your mother, Bliss. I know Aria ain't the best, but you only get one. Youse need to fix this shit, before it's too late."

"No disrespect, Daddy but there's nothing to fix."

"Carlos! I'm here." Aria called from the front door.

"In the kitchen, A." Carlos looked over to Bliss and pointed his finger at her, warning her to be on her best behavior.

Bliss sat back in her chair as her mother approached the table.

"Well, hello everyone!" Aria smiled before taking a seat. Only Carlos and Bentley spoke back.

Carlos looked at Bliss expectantly waiting for her to respond. "Glad you could join us." he spoke up when Bliss wouldn't.

Aria's eyes landed on Bentley. "Who is this?"

"Bentley. Nice to meet you." Even though his girl wasn't talking to her mom, it didn't mean that Bentley didn't have to speak. He did have to say hello, especially since this was not his house.

"Aria. Who are you to my daughter?"

"Her boyfriend."

"Oh?" Aria's eyes shot up. The shock was evident on her face. "Don't you think it's a little soon to be jumping to the next dick dear?"

"Aria?" Carlos warned his ex-wife. He knew that if she kept this up that things would go south very quickly.

"I was just asking. I'm concerned."

Bliss scoffed but didn't say anything else. She had to bite the inside of her lip to prevent from talking period. If she talked, she knew that she would fly off of the handle, and she did not want to upset her father, Or worse, Bentley. She was supposed to be stress free and turning over a new leaf to live a life of calm.

Yeah. Right.

Her mother had one more smart ass remark before Bliss said what the fuck she had to say.

"You seem like something is bothering you, my love. Tell Mommy what it is." Aria smirked at Bliss.

"Oh, for the love of God, would you shut the hell up?" Bliss exploded.

"Scuse us for a second, Carlos." Bentley said, as he grabbed her hand under the table before leading them into the hallway.

"Calm down, and let her talk. You know how ya mother is baby girl, so stop letting her get to you and stop stressing my baby out." Feeling Bentley's touch on her protruding stomach made Bliss relax back into his embrace. "You remember what the doctor said at the last appointment, right?"

It had only been three months since the official start of their relationship, but Bentley was more than Bliss could have ever imagined. He never missed an appointment, and he catered to her every need. He kept that ass in check when she began to get ahead of herself, and he tamed her feisty ass down in only the way that he could.

"Yes, baby, I do."

"A'ight, then." He pecked her lips. "Get that shit together before you stress my baby out."

"She just gets under my skin, Bent! It's like she's just out to get me, and I hate that shit. She purposefully be fucking with me, man. I don't have to deal with that shit, yo." Bliss felt herself getting emotional, but she refused to cry.

"You not here for her, so fuck her, ya feel me? Go in there, hear what ya father gotta say, and then we out. I don't need you stressing and shit, man fa real. I'm liable to kick yo ass and hers. Now, let's get back in here, so we can get the fuck up outta here."

The couple made their way back into the kitchen "Sorry about that, Carlos." Bentley spoke up once he and Bliss were situated. Carlos nodded in appreciation.

"Is that a food baby, or are congratulations in order?" Aria smirked, when Bliss rolled her eyes.

"Why don't you just grow up? Ole childish ass." Bliss bit down on her lip when she realized that she spoke out loud. She looked over to her dad with an apologetic look etched onto her face. "Sorry." Bentley gently squeezed her hand under the table and she knew that she had to do better.

"All I'm saying, dear daughter, is if you're not pregnant then you need to hit the gym, because you've seriously let yourself go." Aria snorted out a laugh. "I mean, my God."

Bliss stood up to leave the table before she could respond with a smart ass remark. She knew that her mom was just being hurtful and a bitch, but she just couldn't shake it and let it roll off of her back.

To be going on six months pregnant, Bliss was absolutely beautiful. She had an angel-like glow to her, and she radiated happiness. Her baby bump was definitely more defined, but she didn't look to be as far along as she actually was; she looked like she was only four months along. She carried the extra weight well and in all the right places. The only thing getting thicker on her was her titties, hips, and thighs.

"I'll just see you later, Daddy."

"Bliss, sit down." Carlos said sternly.

"Look. With all due respect, you want me to sit here and not say a word to her, and that's impossible right now. Especially with her slick ass comments; that's not fair to ask of me, and I don't have to deal with it, so I'm going to remove myself from the situation. My doctor said that I can't be in high stress situations, and this is definitely one of those. Whatever this is about, you can tell me at a later time."

"Ahhh… the moment we've all been waiting for. She makes her grand exit again. It never fails."

"Shut ya mouth Aria." Carlos spoke up. His patience was starting to get very thin. "Bliss. I'm not about to repeat myself." he said to his daughter in a serious tone.

She huffed and puffed, but she sat that ass down, taking her seat next to her man, which was, thankfully far enough away from her mother. She always had a way to get under her skin.

"What is this about, Daddy?" She was beginning to feel restless and was ready to go. She absentmindedly rubbed her stomach, as she waited for her father to explain what was going on.

"Alright, here's the deal. Angel is coming to stay with me for a little while." Bliss' eyes snapped over to her father's. When their eyes met, he gave her a reassuring look.

"What's going on with my baby, Carlos?" Aria asked, sitting up straight in her seat. Her heart rate spiked at hearing the new information.

Bliss mentally smacked her teeth at her mother's dramatics.

"Sin and Lucky are going through some things right now, and it's best if he stays with me for a little while." He turned his attention to Bliss. "I'mma need a little help when I'm at work and everything. For the most part, I'll be working first shift so I'll just need you to get him after school for me, Bliss."

"Why didn't she tell me what was going on?" Aria said, standing up from her chair. "I can keep him. He is my grandchild, too, after all."

"Oh, please." Bliss blurted out before she could stop herself. She did manage to control the eye roll that threatened to take place.

"You have something to add, Bliss?" Aria asked, turning to face Esa.

"Nope." Bliss popped her 'p' for emphasis. She actually had a lot to say, but she wasn't trying to piss her dad off.

"Speak ya mind."

"You act like somebody gonna trust you with they child around that sick animal that you call ya man." Bliss spewed out in one breathe. She watched as her mother's face showed her shock, before her face turned stone cold and void of emotions.

Bliss knew her mother was pissed, but she could really give less than two fucks. "I know I'm not!" Bliss hissed. She sat back in her chair and folded her arms.

"Fuck that's sposed to mean, Bliss? Clue me in here. I feel like I'm missing it." Carlos spoke up from his spot on the counter. He needed her to stop talking in codes and double meanings.

Aria stared her daughter down from across the room. You could feel the heat steaming off of her angry glare. Bliss knew that, if looks could kill, she would have been a tub of melted butter by now.

Bliss stared right back, not backing down one bit. She was so tired of keeping this in. She was tired of the weight being on her. She was tired of being that scared little girl back in her mom's apartment. She tried to keep the thoughts buried, but they slammed into her like a bat out of hell.

*"Shhhhh. It's okay, Ma. Don't be scared. You know I won't hurt you, right? You trust me, baby girl?"*

*Tears spilled over Eleven-year-old Esa's face, as she tried to fight against him. Marcus, her mother's boyfriend, held her arms down by her side as he kissed her tear-stained cheeks.*

*This wasn't the first night that he had snuck into her room. This was just the first night that he had actually touched her. Usually Sin, her older sister, was in here to persuade him not to mess with Bliss, but she stayed out late with a friend tonight.*

*"Shhhh, come on, now, baby girl. You don't want to piss me off, now do you?" she shook her head back and forth feverishly. She saw what he did to Sinaya when she refused him. She didn't want to get hit with his belt.*

*"You better not tell ya mother, either. I swear, I'll kill y'all. She not gone do nothing bout it anyway." he laughed, as he laid on top of a struggling Bliss before forcing his tongue down her throat.*

Carlos slammed his fist down on the kitchen table making the items on it jump up, before clanking down loudly. "Somebody better start fucking talking! And I mean right now!" Carlos yelled.

Bliss jumped when the loud noise caused her to wake up from the trance of her flashback and come back to reality. The memories quickly vanished, but the damage was already done.

Bliss never heard her father raise his voice. You could tell when he was angry, because his hazel eyes would get darker, and his face would be void of emotion. You would never hear him yell or raise his voice, though. Especially not towards his girls.

"I don't know what she's insinuating, Carlos." Aria spoke up after several moments of silence.

Bliss shook her head as she looked at her mom. "Right." She knew right then that she no longer wanted anything to do with Aria. She was officially done with her. "Let me tell you something, Aria. At the end of the day, you are my mother. I have no choice in that, but I do have a choice on how I deal with you. And I choose not to."

"What about your baby, Esa?" Carlos spoke up. He was not a hundred percent sure as to what was going on, but he did know that it broke his heart to hear his daughter say this. He never wanted to admit how fucked up his family was but it seemed like he had no choice but to take notice now. "They deserve to know their grandmother."

"I'm not by any means stopping that. She can have supervised visits with you. Maybe twice a month; we'll work out the details later. I'll even tell her when my baby is born."

"If they even make it that far." Aria chided in.

All the breath left Bliss' body at her mother's words. She felt like she had just been roundhouse kicked in the gut. Before she knew what happened, Bliss was standing over her mother with a stinging hand.

Aria held her stinging cheek, as she watched Bentley come and grab Bliss from standing over her. Hopping up, she tried to reach Bliss over Bentley's shoulder.

"Aria, back up!" Carlos said, trying to defuse the situation. He came and stood in front of Aria, so that she wouldn't try to sneak Bliss. He knew how his ex-wife got down.

"Have you lost your mind?!" he screamed at Bliss. "How dare you put your hands on your mother?!"

"What mother?!" Bliss screamed back. "You never did nothing for me but give birth to me. You let that man rape me. I screamed out for my mom to come and save me, and you didn't do nothing. What kind of mother is that?"

Aria didn't respond as she stared daggers at her daughter.

"You're just a hateful bitch. You can't stand to live in the misery that you created, so you just have to drag everybody else around down with you. Fuck that, and fuck your spiteful ass, too."

Bliss backed away from the pileup and power walked out of the door with her man right behind her.

# Chapter Sixteen

*"Oh, I wanna roll one up, pull my hair up. Got a full cup, don't give a fuck. Oh no, Oh no."*

Bliss and Letty were in the master bathroom singing off key to K. Michelle's "Something About the Night".

Letty was standing in front of the mirror and sink, flat ironing her hair while Bliss was on the floor in front of the floor length mirror laying down her edges to the hair Gods. Her thick hair was in flat twists, so when she took them out, her hair will have big beautiful curls.

Bliss was not in a partying mood. She'd rather stay her pregnant ass home and watch Netflix while snacking on some wings and pickles. However, her person was finally up and moving about, and Bliss needed to be there for her.

"Girl, I can't wait to go out and shake my ass. I gotta shake the cobwebs out!" Letty said in a fit of laughter.

"I know you lying!" Bliss said joining in the laughter. Her phone dinged with a notification. Bliss' smile spread wide, as she read the text from her man. He could be so nasty at times. He had a way of making her blush, even through the phone.

"You heard from Junior?" Letty asked. She hadn't been the best friend that she could be since she had been in her funk so she was trying to play catch up.

"Nah." Bliss answered shortly. "I keep him updated about that baby and shit but he doesn't respond. He reads the messages and keeps it moving."

"That's fucked up." Letty said applying her lipstick.

"I mean, it is what it is. I get why, so I'm not mad; it just is what it is. If the baby is his, he can't say that I wasn't doing my part from the beginning."

"Facts. That is true. I'm proud of the way you that you are handling it though. I would have gone to his house and fucked all his shit up before shooting him in the kneecap."

Bliss snorted out a laugh. "You need some anger management."

"Bitch bye. Don't act like you ain't think about it."

"I don't know what you are talking about. I have turned over a new leaf and am now stress and anger free." Bliss said, trying to sound angelic.

"New leaf my ass. You just slapped ya mama." Letty said through her laughter.

"You got it, yo." Bliss said joining her person in laughter.

*****

"I swear to God! I fucking hate this nigga!" Letty exclaimed loudly as she slammed her phone down on the seat. She and Bliss were riding in the back of an Uber on their way to Club Fantasy.

Letty had been drunk texting Riq since they left their apartment. Bliss rolled her eyes as she outstretched her hand in Letty's direction.

"Give me."

"What? Why?" Letty asked disappointedly.

"I did not drag my pregnant ass out of this house in this tight ass black dress so that you and Riq can argue all damn night long. Now, give me your phone, or I'mma tell him to take me home."

Letty nodded before reluctantly handing the phone over to Bliss. "Fuck him." Letty said, trying to sound convincing, but even to her own ears, it fell flat.

Bliss sighed deeply before turning her attention to the blurry city skyline. *I hope that tonight goes well.*

*****

"Ayyyye!" Bliss laughed out loud, as she encouraged her best friend to twerk on her.

Straightening up, Letty was all smiles, as she wrapped around Bliss. Let was having the time of her life. The alcohol and weed floating through her system had her on ten.

"I'm thirsty." she shouted over the loud music before grabbing Bliss by the hand and leading the way to the bar.

Sipping her Henny-Ale, Letty felt something brush against her neck gently. She began to turn around when a deep voice sexily massaged her ear drums and froze her movements.

"Hello, beautiful."

Goosebumps broke out on her skin as his arms brushed past her own. Before she could gather her thoughts to say a response, he spoke once more.

"Your heart rate went up. What happened? Did I cause that?" He chuckled deeply, causing a river to form in Letty's black thong. She'd know that erotic accent anywhere.

He spun her chair around to face him. The breath got caught in her throat when her eyes landed on Bishop. For the first time in her life, Letty could say that she was speechless.

She smiled shyly. "What are you doing here yo?"

"Well, I'm pretty sure that this is a public establishment." he smirked.

The music was so loud that she had to put her lips right against his ear. "You know what I mean, Bishop!"

"You not happy to see me darling? I know I'm happy to see your sexy ass." Letty giggled before she could help herself. "Let's dance, Ma."

As if on cue "Say It" by Neyo came on, making everybody and their mama jet to the dance floor.

Bliss smiled like a proud mama, as she watched her person be led to the dance floor. She cheesed even harder when Letty started showing Bishop up and dancing for real. She couldn't wait until they got home, because she needed the tea that her best-friend, was obviously holding out on.

"So white boys can dance." She cracked up, laughing, when she realized that Bishop was actually keeping up with Letty. He was really giving her a run for her money.

When Wayne Wonder's voice crooned over the speakers, Bliss bee-lined for the dance floor.

*"Got somebody, she's a beauty. Very special really and truly."*

Bliss sang along as she got lost dancing to the music as she let the smooth beat take over her body. She felt someone approach her and fall in step with her smooth movements.

Normally, she would peek over her shoulder and see who she was dancing with, but she was so wrapped up in her favorite song that it slipped her mind. They were keeping up with her, so she didn't mind. As the song changed, her dance partner wrapped his arms around her and pulled her against his chest.

"Hey, Kitty." Bliss' dance movements halted, instantly, as she snatched away. She tried to walk away when she was pulled back into his chest.

"Get the fuck off of me, Mario!"

"That's how you gone do me?"

"Get off of me, nigga!" She pushed him away only for him to pull her flat against him again. Her small, bulging belly bump rubbed against him.

"You let this nigga get you pregnant, Es? Fuck wrong with you?" Mario asked with a wild look in his eyes. With each passing second, the grip that he had on her arms became tighter and tighter. "So you just don't give a fuck about me no more, huh? It's just fuck Mario?"

She rolled her eyes before pushing him away from her. He came back towards her until he felt a sharp pain in his stomach caused by her knee. "Umph." He bent over as the breath left his body.

"I'mma tell you this one time, and that's the last time I'mma say it a'ight? Leave. Me. The. Fuck. Alone. I don't owe you shit, nigga. The only man I answer to is mine and that's something that you could never be." With that, she sashayed away.

On the outside, Bliss was the perfect picture of calm as she made her way to the entrance of the club. On the inside, her nerves were frayed. She needed to get some fresh air so that she could breathe easily and calm herself down.

Once she was outside, she called her boyfriend to tell him what had just went down. She knew Mario well and knew that he wouldn't stop fucking with her.

"Sup, baby girl? You good?"

"I just ran into my ex."

"I'm on my way. Where you at? Where Letty ass?"

"I'm by the entrance, I stepped outside for some air. Let was dancing last I checked."

"Well, go and find her and then go back to the entrance. Big Black should be there. Stay with him until I get there. I'm not that far away a'ight?"

Her chest felt tight, so she forced herself to take a couple of deep breaths. "Ok, baby."

The line ended, and Bliss went back inside. She went back to the bar in hopes to land eyes on Letty. Walking past the bathroom, Bliss heard her name.

"Es! Over here!"

"Finally, Let. I've been looking for you." Bliss exclaimed, once they were near each other. "We need to go. Bentley is on his way here."

"What's going on? Hold on, I gotta pee like a damn Russian race horse." Letty grabbed Bliss' hand and pulled her into the restroom.

"I ran into Mario."

"Oh, hell no. Where that nigga at? He better be lucky that I don't have my fucking gun. I knew I should have brought that shit." Letty rambled.

"Hopefully, that nigga left. I had to knee his ass in the stomach for him to let go of me. I'm ready to get the fuck up outta here."

"It's a'ight." Letty came out of the stall and began washing her hands. "We bout to go now. Bent should be here, right?"

"Yeah. He said that he wasn't that far away."

"Bet. Come on, let's go."

As the duo began to head to the bathroom exit, a group of five girls entered. Bliss saw them but paid them no mind.

When they got to the door, one of the girls that walked in, spoke up. "Ain't that the bitch that was dancing all over ya man Sheeda?"

Bliss had a feeling that they were talking about her. She and Letty looked at each other with that knowing look. Bliss shook her head, indicating that they just needed to keep it moving. She was having a nice night out, despite the shit with Mario, and she refused to ruin it by dealing with petty bitches.

Letty walked out of the door first, and Bliss was right behind her. Before Bliss could make it all of the way out of the door, she felt her head snap back before she flew backwards.

Several pairs of fist began to heavily rain down on her. Bliss swung her hardest before backing herself up flush against a wall. Scared for her baby's life, Bliss curled around her belly so that she could take the brunt of the hits to her side and back.

She saw that she was surrounded by three of the five girls. She peeped that one girl was teetering and tottering on her six-inch stilettos. Seeing her opening, Bliss kicked that bitch in her shins with her thick heeled shoes, causing her to stumble back and fall and hit her head on the sink.

*One down,* she thought, as she backed herself flat against the wall again. She could handle two bitches easily. She reached out and swung a heavy haymaker at the weaker of the two. The girl she hit was out of breath and barely holding on.

Bliss' fist connected right between the girl's eyes. The bitch's nose began spewing blood, making the girl's hands automatically spring up to hold her nose. Bliss grabbed the bitch by her hair and delivered a devastating knee to her face. As the girl fell down to the ground, she scratched Bliss' face, with her stiletto shaped nails, leaving four red scratches in their trail.

*Another one,* Bliss smirked to herself as she turned her attention to Rasheeda. "Aren't you tired of getting ya ass whooped?" Bliss asked her seriously. "Cause I know I'm tired of beating it. I Preciate the challenge this time, though."

"Bitch, stay the fuck away from my man." Rasheeda swung hard and missed.

Bliss took the opportunity and lunged for the girl's neck. Once her hands locked tight in place, it was game over. Rasheeda struggled to get Bliss off of her but to no avail. She punched wildly, landing punches everywhere on Bliss body. Bliss didn't care, she ate that shit like a full-course meal. As long as her baby was tucked away from the bitch's whack ass punches, she was good. Bliss squeezed tighter, and finally, she felt Rasheeda's body go limp as they slid to the floor.

"Maybe, now you'll stop fucking with me, Bitch!" Bliss said standing up before delivering a kick to the big bitch's ribs and another one to her head. She wanted to spit on that bitch, but she wouldn't allow herself to get out of character, despite the events of the night.

"Esa!!" Bliss heard her name being called before the bathroom door swung open with a loud bang. Bentley came barreling through with two guns drawn and aimed. He looked around frantically until his eyes finally landed on his girl.

He rushed over to her and swooped her up into his arms. "You good, Ma?" he pulled back to look her over. His blood boiled seeing her face scratched and bloody, but luckily, the scratches weren't that deep. "How's my baby? Y'all feeling, a'ight?"

Bliss nodded to answer his questions and ease his worries. "I'm fine baby. I protected my stomach as much as possible."

"Where the fuck that nigga at? He set this shit up, huh?" He gently turned her face side to side to examine it more closely. "Let's go."

"Yeah, he sent his minions in to do it. There were five of them. Where's Letty?"

"She's good; she dusted them other two off. Them bitches is sliced the fuck up."

"She good, though? Where she at?" Bliss was beginning to panic as they walked out of the bathroom. She wouldn't be able to calm down until she laid eyes on her person.

After fighting through the zoo of people, the couple finally made it outside. "Letty!! Where are you?"

"Bliss!! Over here!" Bentley could see a small hand waving feverishly in the air so he steered them in that direction.

Relief washed over Bliss when she saw Letty. Her legs were on autopilot as they carried her the short distance to her person. Her arms wrapped tightly around Letty's neck as they embraced.

"I'm sorry I couldn't get in there, baby girl. At the same they snatched you back in the bathroom, one of them punk bitches sucker punched me. And then it was three bitches on top of me."

"No worries; I was tryna dust them bitches off as fast as possible so I could get to you." Bliss said, finally letting Letty go. She pulled back only enough to survey the damage done to her best friend.

Letty had a black eye, a swollen lip and a few scratches on her neck and arms.

"Look at your fucking face! I swear to God I'm murking every single one of them bitches. They got me on a good night, cause all I had was my damn razor. Otherwise, it'll be a totally different story. yo." Letty exclaimed angrily.

"I'm good. This shit ain't nothing, Ma. I've had worse. Look at your eye Let!"

"I'm good, Esa. I'm just pissed the hell off! Fuck, I can't wait till I see them hoes again."

"You all ready to go?" Bent asked. His nerves were bad and his trigger finger was itching, which was a deadly combination. He couldn't wait to handle Mario bitch ass. "We going to the hospital. I need to make sure my baby alright."

"I got a ride. You gone be ok if I don't go, Esa?"

Bliss smiled knowingly at her person. "Yeah, I'll be a'ight. Handle your business."

"Letty!" Everybody's head turned to the direction from where the call came from. "Come on, son. I'm taking you home." Tyriq said as he approached them.

"No, you are not."

"Look, I'm not in the mood to fucking argue with yo simple ass. Get your ass in the car now."

"You got me fucked up, nigga. I don't know where the fuck you came from, but you can return. Thank you very much." Just then, Bishop came out of the club and headed in their direction.

"You good, baby girl?" He asked Letty once he was right next to her. He placed his arm around her shoulders and tucked her into his side. Letty smiled despite herself and nodded.

"I'm good."

"You ready to go? Gotta put some ice on that eye." He kissed her cheek gently.

"Yo, who the fuck is this clown? You just gone disrespect me to my face Let? That's how we do now?"

"Last I checked Tyriq, you had a baby on the way. Send my congratulations to the misses." She turned to Bishop. "Come on, baby. I'm hungry."

"Anything you want, Little Mama. It was nice seeing you. Maybe next time we can meet under better circumstances." he said to Bentley and Bliss.

"I'll kill you over mine, nigga, so make sure you don't do nothing that'll leave you six feet under." Bliss warned.

"Duly noted," he chuckled. With that, Letty and Bishop walked up the block to his car and pulled off.

"You good?" Bent asked Riq. He felt a little bad, but that wasn't his business. He had his lady. Tyriq nodded but said nothing else. "Aight. I'll holla at you later. I gotta see about my lady and my baby." Bent chunked up the deuce before leading the way for his misses.

# Chapter Seventeen

Bentley unlocked the door to his condo and stepped to the side, allowing Bliss to enter the apartment first. He saw her hesitate a little before finally walking through the door.

She headed right over to his big windows and watched the view of the city. This was her favorite part of his condo. There was just something about the scenic views that calmed her raging mind.

Bentley slowly approached her. He knew that her nerves were frayed, and he didn't want to startle her or give her any reason to feel uncomfortable. When she felt his presence, she turned to face him.

He gently examined her face for the millionth time. Just looking at the scratches made him tight, and he couldn't wait to pump some hot led in that fuck nigga's chest. He was still wound up and on edge, because Bliss didn't want to go to the hospital. He didn't fault her though.

She said that it was because she was tired, but Bentley knew better. He knew that she didn't want to go, because the last time some shit like this popped off, she lost her baby. He could never imagine what that must have felt like. What type of fear that must place inside of you.

Shit, he was feeling that paralyzing fear now. He prayed that everything was ok with their baby, and he told her that he would respect her wishes for right now, but at the first sign of anything wrong, he was hauling her ass Tarzan-style to the damn E.R.

He examined her hands gently. Her knuckles were swollen and there was dried blood all over them. He wrapped his giant hand around her small one before leading her into the kitchen. He sat her on the counter before cleaning her up and giving her an ice pack.

Bentley disappeared down the hallway and returned with a couple of blunts. "Come on." he said over his shoulder. He went outside on the balcony and sat down on one of the beach chairs that he had set up out there.

"So what happened?" he asked after she was situated and he had handed her the blunt. She looked at him like he was crazy. "You can smoke tonight, baby. It's been a long night, and I want you to relax, so smoke." She hesitated for a few seconds while she mulled it over in her head.

Giving in, she took a small pull and began talking. "My song came on so I went on the dance floor. I was dancing by myself, cause Letty was with Bishop. So somebody came up behind me and we danced to the rest of the song. It turns out it was Mario's bitch ass, so I immediately try to leave, you feel me? This nigga kept snatching me up and shit, so I kneed him in his stomach, told him about himself, and walked off." She paused to pass the blunt, "Y'know that's when I called you."

Bentley nodded for her to continue.

"So when I went back in to get Letty, that's when shit hit the fan." Bliss recounted the story for him, blow by blow as they smoked both blunts together. As she finished the story, her eyes watered as the rage took over her body.

"I refuse to lose another child at the hands of that man." She looked Bentley in his eyes, as she said her next words. "I swear, on the life of my baby in heaven, I am going to kill them both without even batting an eyelash or losing any sleep at night."

She willed the tears to stay in, because she was tired of crying over the pain Mario brought to her life. She could not wait to watch the life drain out of his eyes. "I want to hear him beg for his life like I pleaded for my baby's."

*****

"Baby Ben, is that you?" Lita called out from her bedroom, which was located down at the end of the hallway in her small apartment.

Bentley and Bliss went to Lita's house the next day for their weekly Sunday dinner with her. She always went out, soul food style, every week. It was how she kept her family together over the years. You could always work out your problems over good food.

At least, that was Lita's philosophy.

"Who else would it be?" Bentley responded back.

"Maybe the Good Lord blessed a man with directions to my house."

"Cut it out, Lita." Bentley fumed. He didn't play any games when it came to the women in his life.

Lita cackled out a laugh as she made her way down the hallway to her disgruntled grandson. She eyed Bliss' face but didn't say anything. "Oh, quit being a baby, Bent." She kissed his cheek before addressing Bliss. "Hola, Mami."

Bliss kissed Lita's cheek, "Hey gorgeous."

"How's my babies doing today?" Lita ran her hand over Bliss' slightly protruding belly before saying a quick prayer.

Bliss and Lita were actually really close. They developed a close relationship as Bliss frequented Lita's bodega over the years.

Lita was surprised to find out that both of her boys were having problems with the same girl. She could understand why. The King men had been making girls weak in the knees and taking panties off since before time. She knew that her grandsons were handsome. Shit they had her blood running through their veins.

When Bentley finally came and told her what was going on, she understood. She wouldn't dare pick sides between her boys, but she could understand the chemistry that Bentley and Bliss had.

Seeing them together was like watching one soul operate in two beings. She loved how in tune they were with one another. How they moved as one and were always on the same page. She knew Bliss was the one for her Baby Ben.

Lita was reminded of how she used to be with her late husband Vernon. Her heart panged as sadness settled in her heart and spirit. She missed her tall cup of coffee, or Café con Leche as she called him, terribly. She felt incomplete.

Finishing her quick prayer, Lita straightened herself before going over to her fish tank and dropping some food in there.

"We're doing good." Bliss said, as she eyed the big candy jar that Lita kept on her living room table. Lita had all types of candies in there. Bliss made a beeline for her spot on the couch before grabbing the bowl.

"So what I heard is true?" Lita spoke up from the kitchen that was located right off of the living room. "Those bitches jumped you, Amore?"

"They tried to anyway." Bent said, as he joined Bliss on the couch. He placed his feet in her lap before snatching the bowl from Bliss.

"Babe, stop!" she whined, as she poked her lip out. She had been craving some blue raspberry Now & Later's since last night. She was going to punch him if he didn't let her get to them.

"Give that baby the candy, boy."

Bentley smacked his teeth before doing as Lita said. Bliss happily grabbed it, while childishly sticking her tongue out, before sifting through the candy furiously. A small cry of anguish left her mouth as she realized that her candy was not in there.

Bent looked down at her like she was crazy, "Fuck wrong with you?"

"There's no more blue ones." she said with tears pooling in her eyes.

"That's what you bout to cry over?"

"I really wanted some. Can you go and get me some?"

"You dead ass?"

"Yes, baby." she whined.

"You still got mad of 'em in there."

"It's not the same Bent!" She poked her lip out. Why was he being so difficult?

"Just so you know, that shit don't work on me, but I'll go and get them for you."

She genuinely smiled before reaching up to kiss him. "Thank you, baby."

"You're welcome. I'll be back."

After Bentley left, Bliss repositioned and got comfortable on the couch. She pulled out her Mac book and started to do some work. She got some really good shots as always on her and Bent's daily walk.

"Mi, Amore." Lita called out to get Bliss' attention.

"Si, Lita?" Bliss saved her work on the computer before looking over at Lita.

"Did those bitches jump you?" Lita asked calmly.

"Yeah. It's all good though, Lita."

"What's all good? Look at your face, Esa! You're carrying my grandchildren. You can't put yourself in predicaments that can get you hurt or even worse killed, Mija. You have to think better than that. It's no longer just about you, Bliss Esabella Love!" Lita's voice raised higher the more she thought about it. She was ready to go and kick those bitches' ass again. She didn't play when it came to her grandchildren, and she damn sure wasn't going to play that with the lives of her great grand babies at risk. They had her all the way messed up.

Bliss' eyes pooled with tears as Lita's words sunk in. She had to stop putting herself in unsafe situations. She had been very blessed not to have something happen to her baby last night.

She just wanted to go out and support her friend; it was supposed to be harmless fun. None of that shit was supposed to happen. The tears kept pouring the more she thought of the gravity of the situation. Anything could have happened. Anything. What would she have done if she lost this baby too?

Before Bliss could wipe her face, the front door slammed opened.

"What's going on, Lita? Why you yelling?"

Bliss' head snapped over to Junior. Her heart beat wildly against her ribcage, as their eyes connected briefly. She looked away, quickly, ending the brief exchange. Then, she quickly wiped her face and looked at her computer.

Lita broke the awkward silence that ensued. "Bliss has something that she would like to tell you, Mijo." Bliss looked over at Lita like she had lost her mind.

"If it ain't about the baby, then I don't need to hear anything from her."

"Benny, you really need to listen," Lita stressed.

"With all due respect. Lita, it's not your place-" Junior started to say.

"When it comes to the lives of my grandchildren, it is my place!" Lita raised her voice for the second time that day, silencing Junior's arguments once and for all. "She was jumped, Benjamin! Those bitches jumped her, 3-1, knowing that she's pregnant!"

Junior turned sharply to look at Bliss. He was trying to stay calm and not explode, but he was burning with anger. "Why the fuck didn't you call me?!"

"For what, Junior?"

He laughed in disbelief. "Is you dead ass right now yo?" He looked at her incredulously. "It's still possibly my kid, Bliss."

"Don't act like you would've picked up Junior."

He rolled his eyes. "Come on with that sensitive ass shit, man."

"It's the fucking truth, so don't try to put on the 'proud papa' cap now, nigga, cause you in front of Lita. It is what the fuck it is. You not gonna answer so why the fuck would I call you?"

"Who was it? One of his hoes finally got to you?" he smirked at his own joke about his brother.

Bliss gave Junior an exasperated look. "Actually, one of Mario's." She watched as his smirk fell off of his face. "The same annoying ass bitch that keep getting her ass whooped."

"So Mario set this up?" Junior's jaw clenched as the information sunk in. Before Bliss could respond, Junior was heading towards the door. "You know what? Don't worry about it."

"Junior!" Bliss yelled out after him, but the door slamming shut was the only response that she got.

\*\*\*\*\*

Taking the stairs two at a time, Junior was outside in record time. He was on a mission to kill. Rounding the corner of his grandmother's building, Junior's eyes locked in on his target.

His bloodlust overpowered him, as he cocked his fist back and swung. A sinister smile crept onto his face as his fist connected to Mario's face.

Mario was parked in front of Lita's bodega, leaning against his car, before Junior hit him causing him to stumble to the side. "What the fuck?!" Mario called out trying to regain his composure.

Before Mario could react, Junior began raining blows down "Pussy!" Junior spat at Mario. Mario tried to bend down to block the incessant blows, however, the car he was leaning against prevented him from moving.

Junior couldn't control his movements as he delivered the ass whooping that had been building up for forever. His thoughts were clouded by bloodlust as his body moved on autopilot, while Junior delivered blow after devastating blow.

Suddenly, Junior's arms were stuck by his side as his view on Mario became further and further away. When his bloodlust released its hold on Junior, he was able to take in his surroundings. Seeing a fist swing towards him, he tried to dodge out of the way.

The grip around his arms tightened allowing the fists to connect to the side of his face.

"That bitch ass hit," Junior laughed, before he felt the cold of steel against his head. Junior smirked, as he watched the body of one of his attackers fall to the concrete. Bentley had hit the guy across the back of the head with his gun.

Bent aimed his gun towards Junior before firing.

Junior didn't even flinch as the bullet whizzed past his head and impaled its target. Junior stepped away from the dead body of his other attacker before it even hit the ground.

Even if Junior and Bent were not talking, Junior never doubted that his brother loved him. Bentley was the only nigga alive that, when it came down to it, Junior trusted with his life.

Bentley never gave Junior a reason not to trust him, until Junior's mom ended up dead. That was when shit got hazy. Deep down, Junior didn't believe that Bentley killed his mother, Bent loved her just as much as his own.

Looking over at Bent, Junior acknowledged him with a nod. Bent nodded back before tucking his gun and pulling out a burner phone. Bent walked away with the phone glued to his ear.

Junior knew that Bent was taking care of business. Thank God it was dark out, with Bentley just dropping niggas and shit. With the dead bodies being accounted for, Junior stalked over to where Mario pussy ass was still laying down on the ground.

"Getcho bitch ass up, nigga!"

"The fuck is wrong with you, yo?" Mario mumbled through a blood-filled mouth as one of his girls came from around the corner and helped him up.

"Stay the fuck away from her." He kicked Mario in his stomach before turning his attention to the brown-skinned girl standing next to Mario. He stared at her hard before shaping his thumb and index finger into the form of a gun. He placed it against her forehead. "Keep fucking around. This nigga gone lead you to your death."

The way his brown eyes locked onto her freighted stare, he knew he had gotten his point across. His suspicions were confirmed when she began to visibly shake right in front of him. Junior turned his icy stare to Mario before walking away.

He knew he should've killed him right then. *Soon come,* he told his self, *soon come.*

# Chapter Eighteen

"Hello?" Bliss answered her phone.

"Yo."

"What's up, June?" she asked. She was a little surprised that he was calling her.

It had been a little over a month since the last time that they saw each other at Lita's house. Even after what he did to Mario, Junior and Bliss continued to be strained in their relationship.

"You tryna get a slice with me real quick?"

She looked at the clock to check the time, because she had a doctor's appointment today. She was hoping to find out the sex of her mini so that she could start getting the nursery together.

"I don't mind. It's gone have to be quick though. I got an OB appointment today in a few hours."

"A'ight. You mind if I go with you? I'll pick you up."

"Nah that's cool. Give me twenty minutes, and I'll be ready."

"Bet." The line ended, and she looked at Bentley through the bathroom mirror. He was actually smiling at her.

"I'm glad he called you. I didn't want you going to the appointment by yourself."

"Yeah." she sighed. Turning around, she grabbed the avocado oil and began to oil his scalp.

"What's up, baby? Talk to me."

"I'm just skeptical. Me and him aren't on good terms, and I don't know where he fit in my life at."

"You not gone have it all figured out, but today is a start. Go see what he talking 'bout and then, take it from there. Patience is a virtue."

"That we both know I don't possess." she giggled.

"These are facts." He kissed her on her forehead. "Don't stress, baby." He rubbed her stomach lovingly, "Go see about my baby and tell him Daddy said what's up."

She giggled, "You can tell him yourself in about ten weeks."

\*\*\*\*\*

"Here." Junior said handing Bliss a black gift bag. He and Bliss were sitting in his car, in front of her doctor's office, snacking on pizza slices and Now and Laters. Bliss had pickles, too, but Junior said that was doing the most for him. "I got you something."

Bliss put her slice down and wiped her hands before opening the bag. Tears immediately sprang to her eyes as she pulled out the items.

"You ain't even open all of them yet and you already crying." Junior laughed. "Ole sensitive ass baby." He wiped away a few tears that had spilled over.

"Shut up," she laughed.

Bliss pulled out a bunch of clothes and items for the baby. She was floored with appreciation by his gesture. "Thank you, Junior; this means a lot to me."

"There's more."

"Whaaat?" Bliss said in a high-pitched voice, as she pulled out the last gift. It was a long black, jewelry box. Inside of the box, there was a silver locket.

There was a saying in elegant cursive engraved on the locket. The tears started to stream down her face as she read it. *'Handpicked for earth, by my sister in heaven.'*

"Oh, Junior." she said through her tears. She was overcome with emotion.

"Open it." Junior urged. Bliss followed his instructions and began crying even harder. On the inside, there were two sonogram pictures. One was of her baby girl Cielo, and the other was the first picture of the baby that she was carrying now.

"Junior. This is beautiful. Thank you." She reached over and hugged him.

While in the embrace Junior spoke up. "I didn't want you to think that I didn't care about the baby."

"I don't think that. I know this whole situation is a lot to deal with."

"I'm sorry, Ma, for how I treated you. I knew what it was when Bent showed up to the cookout that day. I just couldn't leave you alone, and I wanted you to myself." Junior ended the hug so that he could look her in her eyes. "When you got pregnant and told me how far along you was I was a happy man. I'm not gone lie. But I knew at the doctor's office when he said nine weeks that the baby wasn't mine."

Bliss looked down at her hands as she listened to Junior.

He lifted her chin with his finger so that she would look at him. "No matter how the results come back, you and the baby are going to be a part of my life. I know I'mma be wrapped around shorty's finger whether they call me uncle or daddy." he laughed.

Bliss felt like the weight of the world had been lifted off of her shoulders and heart.

"I'm glad to have my friend back." she said with tears in her eyes. She really did miss her best friend, and she was glad to know that he was willing to be a part of her life.

Junior looked over at her and smiled, genuinely, "Me, too."

\*\*\*\*\*

"Hey, baby!" Bliss answered Bentley's phone call cheerfully. She and Junior were having a good day. After her doctor's appointment, Junior decided to take Bliss shopping for more baby clothes.

"Aye." Bentley said into the phone. "Where you at?"

"Junior wanted to go and get some thing's for the baby so we went to the Children's Place on Flatbush. I got some news, baby." She said happily.

"Listen, Bliss," Bentley said. "Lita shit just got robbed. Tell Junior to bring you to the crib. I don't want youse out."

"What?" Bliss stopped walking to listen more carefully to what he was saying. Her heart sank to the pit of her stomach.

"What's wrong?" Junior asked, noticing the change in Bliss' demeanor. He checked his phone and saw that he had mad missed calls from Bentley, and an unknown number.

"Is she alright?" Bliss questioned Bentley.

"Hell, nah. I can't even stay at the store and shit, cause they fucked her up." Bliss' breath caught in her throat, hearing the news. "They took her to the hospital by ambulance. I had to stay back and lock the rest of the store up. I'm on my way there now."

"What's going on, Esa?" Junior asked again. He was becoming impatient; he hated to be left in the dark.

"It's Lita." she rasped out. "They robbed her. Bent said that she's in the hospital."

"Fuck you mean? Who fucking robbed her?" Junior felt his blood began to boil. "Man, let's go." He started to walk, quickly, towards his car. He was a few feet away from Bliss when he noticed a car speeding down the block. When the car got closer to them, it slowed down to a slow crawl.

Everything moved in slow motion as his instincts kicked in. He double backed to get back to Bliss.

"Junior, what's wrong?" Bliss asked noticing his facial expression.

"Get down, Bliss! Now!" he yelled out before he threw his body over hers as a shield. "I got y-" was all he could get out before bullets started to spray them.

**Tat-tat-tat-tat-tat-tat-tat**

The bullets forcefully tore through Junior's body causing him and Bliss to crash to the ground.

Bliss' heart was beating out of her chest as she tried to comprehend what was going on. It felt as if she could feel her heart beating in her throat when she heard footsteps approaching. She closed her eyes and played dead as the footsteps stopped close to her.

**Tat-tat-tat-tat**

She bit her lip to keep from screaming, as she felt Juniors body jump up as more bullets pierced through his flesh. She heard the footsteps fade away before hearing the tires to a car screech.

With each second that passed, Bliss could feel Junior's body getting heavier and heavier.

"Bliss! Answer me, baby! Can you hear me?" Bentley yelled through the phone. The only answer he got in return was Bliss' ear piercing, unsettling scream.

"Junior!"

**To be continued...**